VICTORY STREET

Richard MacSween

Ⓐ

Andersen Press • London

For Helen

First published in 2004 by
Andersen Press Limited,
20 Vauxhall Bridge Road, London SWIV 2SA
www.andersenpress.co.uk

British Library Cataloguing in Publication Data available

ISBN 1 84270 361 7

Cover photographs © 2004 by Emma Jones
Cover design by Rebecca Garrill

Typeset by FiSH Books, London WC1
Printed and bound in Great Britain by Mackays of Chatham Ltd.,
Chatham, Kent

1: Someone Else's Shoes

1

Angi's singing along to the radio. That's a good sign. She's doing some cooking. So's that. It can only mean one thing.

'Who's the lucky guy, then?' I ask.

'Sorry?'

'You will be. It's not him who came in the shop today, is it?'

'Who you on about, Ellie?'

Try again: 'Him with glasses that spent hours reckoning to look at the writing desk.'

'He didn't just look at it; he bought it.'

'You what?' I shout and jump up. 'He's bought it?'

I'm straight through the connecting door and into the shop.

'Well, as good as,' Angi shouts behind me. 'He's coming back tomorrow.'

Relax, Ellie, for two reasons. For one, because the writing desk's still there, gleaming faintly in the dark of the shop, and for two, because Angi never learns that when customers said they're coming back it's only because they don't want to hurt her. For some reason she believes them.

She's the same with boyfriends.

I push past the manky bedside cabinet with the drawer front coming off and put my hand on the top of the writing desk. I just want to touch it, make sure it's still here. It only arrived yesterday but I love it.

It's the only thing in the shop with any class about it. Everything else is cheap plywood or chipboard or basic treewood. Doors hanging off, drawers that stick, handles missing, chairs too new to be antique but too old to be new, a glass-topped table that must have been stylish twenty years ago but now just looks stupid. Who wants a table made out of glass?

This is our shop, the junk shop, though Angi calls it 'an antique shop'. In fact, I call it an antique shop too, if anyone asks. I just hope they don't come round to look. But why would they?

Matty comes into the shop.

'Whozat?' he asks, looking at the door.

And there *is* somebody standing in the doorway, peering in, and it gives me a shock. I don't know why it should, there's always folk lurking in the shop doorway, shading their eyes under a hand to see better into the shop, or just sheltering from the rain. Later you get couples kissing and groping. Last week I heard water running and went into the shop to catch this guy taking a leak. I put the light on and he put his thing away so fast pee went everywhere. Served him right.

The man out there now must be the new boyfriend.

'It's locked,' I shout. 'We're shut.'

He looks puzzled, what I can make out of his face.

'You'll have to go round to the back door.'

He doesn't move. Honestly! Angi picks some.

'Back – door!' I shout in my talking-to-an-idiot voice. He goes off.

'Whozee?' asks Matty.

'Mum's new boyfriend,' I tell him.

'Azee gone awready?'

'You're learning fast, Matty. No, he's just gone round the back.'

Matty grins up at me, little fatface.

'Story later?' he asks.

'Yeah,' I say. 'Story later,' and give him a hug. We go through to the back. I'm waiting for the knock at the back door, but nothing happens.

Angi's getting some burgers out of the freezer. When I said she was doing some cooking I didn't mean anything special.

'I sent him round to the back door,' I say.

'Mmm?' says Angi, pretending she's not bothered either way.

'He was at the shop door, your new boyfriend.'

Angi stops what she's doing. Some frozen peas fall out of the freezer and roll across the floor.

'Ellie,' she says. 'I don't know who you're on about. If you must know, I *am* meeting someone later…'

'Surprise, surprise!'

'But he's not coming round here.'

'So who's that at the shop door?'

'How should I know? I'd be grateful if you'd mind your own business, thank you very much!'

When Angi's mad she tries to go into this posh voice. But now I'm mad too.

'Well, maybe it is my business. I suppose you want me to look after Matty.'

'Hey!' says Angi. 'If you don't want to, that's okay. I'll ask Lewis.'

'Oh yeah! I'm sure Lewis'll want to stop in.'

Lewis is my older brother, half-brother. He's always out these days, in pubs or somewhere.

'Well, Matty,' says Angi. 'Looks like no one wants to stay in with you tonight. Will you be all right on your own?'

The things she says! Matty blinks up through his specs at us.

'Angi! That's terrible! I didn't say I didn't want to. I just meant you can't assume.'

'Eleanor, if you don't want me to go out, just say.'

'But I'm not saying that!'

'Well, no. Because you seem to want to pair me off with somebody who just happens to be lurking in the shop doorway.'

'I thought . . . ' I begin to say.

But it's a waste of time. What can you say when people get it wrong on purpose? Not 'people'. Angi, that's who I'm talking about. My mother.

*

6

I had a careers interview today with Mr Ash, the careers teacher. That's a laugh for a start: what do teachers know about careers?

Anyway, when it's my go, I can't think of anything. I ought to say I'd like to be a social worker because it's me who looks after Matty, and Angi. We're talking serious, full-time responsibility here. But of course I don't say it.

'So . . .' says Mr Ash. 'Got any ideas at all, Eleanor?'

He sticks a finger in his ear and swivels it round.

You have to feel sorry for Mr Ash, nicknamed So-So because he starts every sentence with 'so'. They make him sit here all day talking 'careers' with a stream of kids who'll be lucky to get jobs shelf-stacking in Asda. He looks at the end of his finger to see if he's scored any wax. It's just too depressing.

Then I realise I'll have to say it, what I want to be.

I can't stop thinking about yesterday's delivery of new stuff to the shop, new *old* stuff, if you know what I mean. After Imran and Angi had unloaded it – Imran helps Angi with moving stuff when he's not busy – I went and investigated. The furniture's rubbish, like I say, but sometimes interesting things have been left in it: coins down the back of settees, old photos in drawers. Even the newspapers lining the drawers are old enough to be a worth a read.

Once I found what I thought was a dead rat in the bottom of a wardrobe. It still had its face on and paws, and Angi told me it was a fox stole. She said old women used to wear them round their necks. I thought she was making it up but it was good enough for Matty who

7

immediately wrapped it round his neck. Angi said he'd get some horrible disease off it but she didn't do anything about it. That's Angi for you.

But the most interesting thing about this latest load of junk was the writing desk.

I was over like a shot. Imran helped me work out how it opened, pushing in the two buttons so the front opened up. There's a leather bit to write on and at the back rows of neat little drawers, each with a little brass ring to open it. Of course, I'm into them straight away, thinking there's going to be sovereigns and stuff, but there was only a wooden bobbin with a bit of scarlet thread on it, a few paper clips, a couple of pebbles and a rubber band so perished it snapped as soon as I twanged it.

Then I tried the big drawers below: old newspapers from the Second World War, all writing and hardly any photographs; some music all coming apart, *Chopin Mazurkas* it said on the front – I've heard of Chopin but what's a mazurka? Underneath all that was a book.

I pulled it out. It had a lovely deep blue cover and on it, in a fancy font in gold letters, it said *Minute Book*. Inside it was completely blank. I didn't know what it meant: which 'minute'? Whose minute?

'Should come in handy,' said Imran behind me. 'For doing your accounts.'

'Don't have any to do,' I said.

'Everybody's got accounts to do,' said Imran. 'Incomings and outgoings, innit.'

I put the minute book back in the drawer and closed up the top of the writing desk.

8

And now, sitting across from Mr Ash, I say: 'I want to be a writer.'

He looks hard at me. He's trying to work out if I'm being serious. I know for a fact that Paula Cannon said she wanted to go into advertising and before her Jamie Orlando put in a bid to be a TV chef. He thinks being called Jamie is a good start. Mr Ash asked him if he knew a chicken's arse from its elbow. There's no need for that. Jamie came out trying to convince himself he could make a modern apprenticeship if he's really lucky.

'So, how you doing in English, Eleanor?' he asks me now, as if that's got anything to do with it.

'All right. We've spent a million years doing *Roll of Thunder*.'

'Right.' He doesn't know what I'm talking about, of course. Mr Ash is geography. 'So, what kind of writing?'

'Oh, stories,' I say. I've read enough of them – you can read a hundred books in the time it takes to study one at school – and most nights I make a story up with Matty, so what's the problem? But to be honest, what appeals is seeing myself sitting at the writing desk, with a lamp above me, writing words slowly and steadily, looking up from time to time when I'm trying to think of the right word, and then when I've thought of it, writing the word down, the dark blue ink flowing out of the nib of the fountain pen – it's always a fountain pen I think of – the words slowly covering the page, each word a leap into the dark...

'So, what've you written so far, Eleanor?' asks Mr Ash.

Arsehole. Why's he think he's got to try and catch me out?

'Oh, stuff,' I say. As soon as I get out of here, I'm going to start. Tonight. As soon as I get home. As soon as Matty's sorted out. Soon.

'Hmm. Look, Eleanor, your GCSE predicted grades are pretty good, so you could do A levels. Think about what you want to do.'

'I've thought about it. I know.'

'Okay. So what you going to write about?'

I stand up.

'Well, not this place. That's for sure.'

And walk out.

Lisa Kildare's waiting outside.

'So, how'd it go, Ellie?' she asks.

'Oh, so-so,' I reply.

It's not funny any more but it's a gag everyone's got to do.

2

Angi's gone out now.

We're talking again. She asked me if she looked okay. I told her she looked great. But she just looks like she always does when she's going out: make-up the same as when she first started slapping it on back in the 1980s or whenever, and as usual she's showing her legs off. You can see how Angi turns heads, but they don't stay turned. Legs isn't everything.

I've done Matty's story. It's always monster stories we make up. These days I don't even ask what kind of story he wants, I just ask what the monster's called. Tonight he says: 'Splodoosh.'

'Where's he live?'

'Splodoosh.'

'Figures, like the Americans live in America. Let's

call it Splodooshia; it sounds more like a country.'

'Nah. Snot a country.'

'Oh, right. So what is it?'

'Tsa lake.'

'Well, it's a good name for a lake, Splodoosh. Who else is in the story, Matty?'

'Errr...'

This is where it always gets tricky, character number two. Sometimes we never get a second character, and the monster has to eat breakfast, or watch TV, or smash entire cities, all by itself.

'Dog,' he says. 'Called Spot.'

Ah well, even the best have to borrow sometimes.

Anyway, Splodoosh and Spot tear themselves away from watching underwater TV long enough to go to outer space and splat some even worse monsters. It's not one of our better efforts, but Matty seems contented enough. I leave him playing with his toy car, his 'brum-brum', driving it up and down the quilt, and go up to my room and read for a while.

My room is the attic, which is freezing in winter and roasting in summer, but at least it's my own room. I keep the skylight open to let the heat out and some air in. It also lets in the street sounds: people talking, music spilling out of The Green Dragon, the black binbag that's stuck on the TV aerial crackling in the slightest wind. I'm developing a theory that the angle of the skylight is all-important: if it's open on the fourth hole it bounces the sounds into the attic just right, like a satellite dish picking up the signal, keeping me in touch with the street even when I'm up in bed.

After a couple of chapters I go down to check Matty: he's fast asleep with the light still on, his fat face in a dreamy smile.

And now, finally, I can go down to the shop, open the writing desk.

I spoke to Mr Carmichael today. He was my English teacher for the first two years at Northend High and though he doesn't teach me now he was the one who got me into reading. It was Mr Carmichael who showed me an escape route when Angi and Matty and Victory Street all got too much, when I wanted to get the world out of my face. Open a book, he said, get lost in that. Mr Carmichael, my lifesaver.

I said: 'What do you need to write, Sir?'

I meant grades, but he said: '95% perspiration, 5% inspiration, that's what they say.'

'Well,' I said, 'I know about perspiration – thank you very much – but what about the missing 5%?'

'"Inspiration" means "breathing in", it's not something you have within you. You get it from outside, all round you like air. Just breathe in.'

'Just breathe in?' You can never tell if he's being serious.

'As opposed to "expiring", which means "breathing out".'

'I thought it meant dying, Sir.'

'It does. The time you expire and fail to inspire, you're dead.'

'Thank you for explaining that, Sir. How's it help me write?'

'Just breathe in.'

And he's off down the corridor to bollock Ganja Greenwood. Thank you, Mr Carmichael.

I get the lamp from the back room, balance it on top of the writing desk and switch off the shop light. Everywhere's dark now except for this little tent of light where my hands hold the minute book. I open it. Inside the front cover is printed: *Foolscap*, *Feint*. Two more strange words. The pages are off-white, slightly creamy, and the lines running across *are* faint, faint blue, though you'd have thought they'd have known how to spell it.

I don't think anyone's ever opened this book before. I stare at the blank page, and keep staring.

I can't think of anything to say.

It's as if the blank page is a dare, and it's dared all the words out of my head.

And then, because I told myself I was going to do it, I write a word. *Eleanor*. Then: *15*. And then: *Writer*.

Underneath *Eleanor* I write *Matty*. And then I stop, surprised at myself. Matty, before Angi? Your brother before your mum? Then I think, well, if that's what my pen wants to do, who am I to stop it? Writing's writing, not thinking. And I say to my pen (which I have to point out is not the classy fountain pen I'd imagined, because I haven't got one – slight drawback there – but a bog-standard biro), I look my pen in the eye (it's like an eye if you look straight at the point) and say out loud: 'Carry on, you're the boss.'

It doesn't take long to get halfway down the page, and okay, it's only a list of people I know and a bit about

14

them, and I don't know what Mr Carmichael would say
but I'm doing pretty good at breathing, both ways.

Eleanor	*15*	*Writer.*
Matty	*10*	*Brother, favourite, actually half-brother.*
Angi	*37 (I think)*	*Mother. Love her really.*
Dad	*40ish*	*Steve, now married to Auntie Sue.*
Lewis	*18*	*Half-brother. Ignores us mostly.*
Matty's Dad	*Youngish*	*Gets called Matty's Dad.*
Anna	*15*	*Lives next door, over hairdressing shop, best friend, sarcastic.*
Muzz	*16*	*Lives next door the other way, over Asian shop. Real name Mushtaq, I think.*
Lewis's Dad	*?*	*Used to visit.*
Imran	*30ish*	*Muzz's brother, drives a taxi and helps Angi do removals.*
Daz	*15*	

I stop there because I'm about to start putting down
everyone in my class. I cross out *Daz 15* and then feel
bad about crossing him out. ~~*Daz 15*~~. It's not his fault.

Why've I bothered putting in Lewis's dad? I haven't
seen him for years and I don't think Lewis has either.
Nobody cares about him.

The kitchen door opens.

15

Angi? Back so soon? It's not been a good night.

I put the minute book back in its drawer, unplug the lamp and take it into the back room.

Angi's already flat out on the settee, staring at the ceiling. She looks tired.

'You're early,' I say.

'Yes, pet. Make us a tea, will you.'

I switch the kettle on. I'm going to have to ask.

'How was it?' I say.

'Okay.'

What's that mean? But she doesn't want to talk.

Then she says: 'He didn't turn up. Must have been me, got the time wrong or something. But I got chatting to this guy, bought me a drink. Invited me to ring him.'

'You can't! Some loser you happen to bump into!'

'Suppose not,' she says, then: 'Might do, all the same.'

She's crazy. Since Matty's dad left, Angi's forgotten the rules. She can always get men interested but she's too keen; she scares them off. She even brings them home the first time. I come downstairs in the morning to find Matty chatting away to total strangers. Usually they don't hang around for long.

'What've you been doing?' Angi asks. 'Matty go to bed all right?'

''Course he did.'

I don't say what I've been doing. I can see she's thinking about why her date didn't show, and how bad will it be if she rings the new guy tomorrow.

'I haven't been doing anything,' I say.

3

Me and Muzz are out on Victory Street, just chatting, when this battered red car appears at the end of the street, driving fast. It slows up at the speed bump. There's four lads in it, white lads, I don't know them, and the one in the passenger seat shouts at me: 'Paki shagger!' And they drive off, waving v-signs at us. Along the street they chuck a cigarette packet at an Asian woman.

Muzz shouts after them: 'Well, int she the lucky girl?' but they're gone.

It's what you get in this town, that kind of idiot stuff, but they don't usually drive down Victory Street doing it.

I don't know what victory the street was named after, but it can't have happened round here. Defeat, more like; draw at best. It's a bus ride into Boltby town centre or a long walk. People only come out to Northend if they have to.

We're standing across from our shop, *Angi's Antiques*. Next to it is Muzz's shop, *Aslam's General Store and Grocery*, and next to it on the other side, Anna's mother's hairdresser's, *Hair Today*.

I once pointed out to Muzz that a general store *included* groceries so it didn't need to be called 'general store *and* grocery'.

He said: 'Okay, so I'll tell my uncle to change it to *Aslam's General Store Which Of Course Includes Groceries*.'

I said: 'And Kids' Toys.'

He said: 'And Emergency Samosas.'

I said: 'And Soft Porn.'

He said: 'We don't!'

I said: 'Don't let your mum look inside them magazines you sell; she'll have a fit.'

He said: 'I know what; we'll leave the shop name as it is now.'

I said: 'Best thing.'

We're okay, me and Muzz. Sometimes when it's raining we go in the storeroom at the back of his shop and chat or play cards.

There's sacks of rice and chapatti flour, and even chilli powder in bags as big as sofa cushions and you know how hot chilli powder is; boxes of vegetables that are past it, onions growing green shoots, wizened peppers, potatoes putting out roots that quiver as though

18

they're alive, which I suppose they are. Sometimes Muzz's grandad comes in and says something to Muzz in Punjabi, and Muzz goes off dutifully and does whatever it is. Muzz's grandad's face is shrivelled as an old yellow pepper and his beard is dyed red with henna. I don't think he knows much English.

We watch the red car go down the street, screech off round the corner. Then a black car appears and even from here we can hear the bass of whatever sound system they've got in there. The thump-thump comes up through my feet.

The black car comes slowly up Victory Street. It's got tinted windows so you can't see in. It stops next to us.

God, they must be deaf.

The windows come down. It's Taj, who Muzz says is a cousin. The difference is where Muzz is an all-round great guy, Taj is a complete prat. He acts like he's got the contract for the whole area and it's not Northend but the Bronx. He's seen too many movies, and he hasn't twigged they're just movies, made up. He thinks Ali G is for real.

'Hi, Bro!' he says to Muzz. He ignores me of course, which suits me fine, though the guy in the back seat is giving me the eye, chewing gum.

'Hi!' says Muzz, and they shake hands, this big buddy-buddy production number.

'Skinhead bastards about,' says Taj. 'Watch yourself, Muzzy.'

'Yeah, right,' says Muzz. 'A car just went by, didja see them? Gave Ellie some pain.'

'It's you we're looking out for, man, not Ellie.'

'Yeah, but . . . '

'Muzz! Why'd they diss Ellie? Eh?'

Muzz says nothing.

'You know why. Cause of *you*, man.'

Muzz knows this is true, but.

'It's still her what they shouted at,' says Muzz.

Good on you, Muzz.

Taj shakes his head in despair. He's got these really carefully shaved sideburns that must take him hours to get so sharp.

'You know best, Muzz. See you round,' he says.

And he drives off. But just before he does, the guy in the back who's been staring at me says, right in my face: 'Bitch!' and they're off down the street, thump-thump.

'Anyone else got any comments?' I shout after them.

It's nothing new, but this time it really gets to me, first the red car and then the black. It's just me and Muzz chatting, for Chrissake!

Muzz puts a hand on my shoulder to comfort me, and Angi comes out of the shop.

'What's going on, Muzz? Is she all right?' she calls across.

'What is it with everyone?' I shout. 'Why do they have to talk to me through Muzz?'

I'm totally hacked off with everyone now.

'Nothing wrong with her, obviously,' says Angi, huffily, and goes back in. *She's* in a bad mood now! 'Come and mind the shop while I go to the supermarket.

If you can spare the time,' she shouts at me before she disappears inside.

The battered red car's coming back up the street. I've had enough.

'See you later, Muzz,' I say and follow Angi into the shop.

Angi's in the back, getting her coat. Matty's watching a video.

'I've got a lift with Imran,' she says, 'but he's going now. Won't be long!' And she's off.

I wander back into the shop. Nobody's going to come in because it's late Thursday afternoon, nearly teatime. A dead time. I could read my book, or get the minute book out and do some writing. What about though?

Maybe something in the shop'll inspire me. That hatstand. That table with round marks where somebody's left a hot mug on it. That chamberpot.

Really inspiring.

That wardrobe. This growling noise starts up inside it, getting louder. And louder. There's a scratching sound, something pushes at the door and the whole wardrobe rocks backwards and forwards. The growling is more like roaring now, and the door suddenly bursts open and this huge, smelly lion dives out of the wardrobe, mouth wide open, mane having a bad hair day – and it's coming straight at me!

Only kidding.

Have you read it, that one? No need to write it again then, is there?

The doorbell rings and a man walks in. Though it's a

warm day, he's wearing a black leather coat.

'I wonder if you could help me, young lady,' he says. 'This is Angi's Antiques, is it?' He says the shop name like it's a bit silly; I know what he means.

'Yeah,' I say. 'That's right. But she isn't in.'

'That's a pity,' he says. 'I was hoping to catch her. The lady herself.' This is Angi he's talking about so I'm struggling not to laugh.

'Yeah. Well, she won't be back for a while.'

'Mind if I take a look round, see what you've got?' But he doesn't seem very hopeful.

'Okay, fine.'

Then he says: 'A bit young to be left in charge, aren't you?'

Creepy.

I say: 'Oh, I'm not on my own. There's Matty in the back room.'

I try to say Matty's name as if he's twenty-five and does weight-training. I just hope his video doesn't end and he comes in. But it's okay because the cartoon voices keep going.

A bit of a giveaway, the cartoon voices.

'Hmm.' He stares a moment, then starts looking round. 'Like it, do you, living here?'

I'm confused. 'It's okay, over a shop, do you mean?'

'No, I meant this area. Rather a lot of our coloured friends.'

Here we go! Every so often someone comes in and they say something like: 'It makes a change to hear English spoken.' They're just testing, and you know if

22

you said what they wanted to hear, they'd start: *Paki* this, and *immigrant* the other.

But this is a shop; we've got to sell things. So we don't encourage them, but you can't fall out with them. They wouldn't buy anything, they'd never come back.

I don't have time to think of a reply. Bang on cue, Muzz comes in.

'They've smashed up Taj's uncle's shop!'

'Who?

'Don't know. Could be those guys in the red car. They came back.'

'What d'you mean – "smashed it up"?'

'Bricked both windows.'

The customer butts in. 'Lot of trouble round here, is there?'

Muzz stares at him. 'Not if we got left alone, no. Except for Javed of course, who's a thousand per cent psycho.'

'Well, there you go then,' says the customer. 'Maybe it's your lot's fault. Maybe you're asking for it.'

Muzz stares a bit harder. I know he wants to really put this guy straight, but he knows he can't, not in our shop.

Muzz is usually broad Lancashire, but he can do this brilliant Pakistani accent and that's what he drops into now. 'Asking for it? How is that, please? Who is being foolish enough to ask for it?'

'It's an expression, an English expression,' says the man to Muzz, Muzz who's going to score an A starred in English. 'You wouldn't understand...'

Then he twigs what Muzz is doing and dries up.

23

Muzz says: 'Got to go. These English expressions are just beyond me.'

As he goes out, Taj and his mates screech past in the black car. Things are getting jumpy round here.

'Anyway,' the customer says, 'I can't wait all day. Give this to Angi; tell her to give me a bell.'

He gives me a little card. It reads:

ST GEORGE TAXIS
proprietor: Norman Parks
weddings, airports, ect
01393 660066
'Parks' you where you want to be!

On the card there's a little drawing of St George, I suppose it's meant to be, killing the dragon.

'That's myself,' he says, pointing at the card. 'Norman Parks.'

I say: 'You've spelt "etc" wrong.'

He says: 'It's short for "ec-setera", so it's ee cee. Latin, I think you'll find.'

No point in arguing with him.

'Anyway,' he says, 'tell your cocky little mate to watch his step. We can't have the natives getting uppity.'

And he's off, giving me a little wave as he walks past the window.

Matty comes into the shop behind me.

'Whaz for tea?'

'Oh, let's see what Angi brings back from Asda. Might be something nice.'

24

'Biscuit for now.'

'Yeah. Why not, Matty.'

I need some fun. As soon as Angi gets back, I'll call for Anna; she'll make me laugh.

4

We're watching the crowd round Taj's uncle's shop. They're angry and they're arguing, mostly in Punjabi but with a bit of English mixed in. Muzz is in there somewhere, helping with the argument. Both of the shop windows have these big jagged holes in them. Taj's aunt is sweeping up the broken glass.

'Lucky women,' says Anna. 'They get to do the clearing up. The men have it tough – they've got to do the bawling and shouting! What is there to argue about? Some bastards smash your windows. If you knew who it was, you'd go and sort them out, but nobody knows, so forget it.'

She's not the most sympathetic person in the world, Anna isn't.

'Muzz thinks it was those lads in the red car.'

'Yeah,' says Anna. 'Whatever. There's more where they came from. God, Ellie, this town! How do you stand it?'

I shrug. 'Just live here, I guess.'

I've lived here all my life, so I don't think about how a different place might be, but Anna's moved around. She hasn't been on Victory Street long; she was in a little village before.

'Look at that!' she says, pointing. 'Closed circuit TV, keeping an eye on what? A bomb site.'

She's right. There's a TV camera on top of a long pole, aimed down and moving slowly round. There used to be a mill here but it got demolished leaving an empty space with piles of bricks and rubble round the edges.

'In fact,' she says, 'the camera's the only thing worth nicking; they ought to get another, and then they could keep an eye on each other.'

I say: 'There must have been something worth pinching from the shop.'

'How do you make that out?'

'Well, didn't they?'

'What? A roll of glittery sari material? Like, that's what all fashionable skinheads are wearing this season. Ellie, they just wanted to smash it up. They didn't nick anything.'

A dog crossing the waste ground yelps as some kids pelt it with stones.

'One way to get your kicks: stone a dog,' says Anna. 'Still, look at us, standing here watching an argument in a language we don't know. I'll die if I don't get out.'

That's the difference between us. I know what she means, but I don't want to go anywhere. I live here.

'Ellie, I never told you!' says Anna, suddenly remembering. 'I caught a couple of lads giving Matty a hard time yesterday.'

'He never said. What happened?' I ask her.

'He's sitting on our shopstep, playing with his brum-brum and these two lads come by and Matty looks up and grins at them. One of them says something. They stop. I'm not really paying attention, I'm inside the shop, tidying up the magazines. Then Matty stands up and gives one of these lads a big hug, like he does. I'm watching now. The lad sort of backs away, it's like embarrassing for him, he's, I don't know, nineteen or twenty, and this is Matty, a kid with a runny nose. But then the lad hugs him back. And I think: *Ah! That's nice*. And go on with the tidying up – there's a *Vogue* been dropped under the seat. *Vogue*, in Boltby; dream on! But when I come back up, they're still hugging, and then I see that Matty's stopped hugging and it's only the lad who's doing the hugging and he's doing it harder and harder. And I'm like: *Shit me!* and run outside. Of course, he lets Matty go straight away when I'm stood in front of him, blazing. But when I ask him what the fuck he thinks he's doing, he doesn't even look sorry, just says: *Should be in a home, a kid like that. Look at that: snot all over my jacket!* And then he says: *Or maybe he should have been put down at birth. Hitler had the right idea!* And they walk off. I was gobsmacked, Ellie. What d'you say?'

She's not asking me of course because there's nothing to say.

''Course I'm not gobsmacked for long. I'm holding an aerosol and I throw it. It hits him in the middle of his stupid back. But he just laughs and turns round: *We'll be cleaning up round here, getting rid of the filth. Soon: I'm warning you.* What's he mean, Ellie?'

I shrug. Right in front of me Taj's aunt picks up a long splinter of glass; it's as long as her forearm. As she lifts it, the light catches it and it shines like the blade of a sword. She could be going to war.

I say: 'Maybe his mates have started already, "cleaning up". Maybe smashing up Asian shops is what they mean.'

Taj drives up. He's got the music switched off, so it must be serious. He and his mates pile out of the car and join in the arguing.

Muzz comes over.

'So what's the big dispute?' I ask.

'Taj reckons he knows who's done it. He says he's going to sort them out.'

'Why doesn't he just go and do it, then?' asks Anna.

'Too simple, man,' says Muzz. 'Taj has to be persuaded not to do something first, *then* he goes and does it, just to show no one's going to tell him what to do. We have a word for a person like that.'

'Let me guess,' says Anna.

Taj and his mates start getting back into the car. One of them looks across and gives us the finger.

'Mate of yours, Muzz?' Anna asks him.

'Nothing to do with me!' says Muzz. 'Jumping to conclusions, are we? "All you Pakis" or something like that?'

'Sorry,' says Anna.

'Since you ask,' says Muzz, 'I think he's my uncle's cousin's son or something, but so what? He's a waste of space!'

'Anyway,' says Anna, 'enough excitement for one day. That TV camera looks exhausted with all the action.'

We all look up and watch it swivel round, silently, taking it all in, like a tall bird.

'Want to go out Saturday night, Ellie?' asks Anna.

'Could do,' I say. 'I'll check if Mum needs me.'

'Sorry, Muzz,' says Anna putting a hand on his arm. 'It's a girl thing. Strictly no Y chromosomes.'

I didn't know she paid so much attention in school.

'Y?' says Muzz.

He's a sweetie.

We walk back down Victory Street. The sky's grey, but it's still muggy and warm.

'I'll ring you about Saturday,' I tell Anna, and turn into our shop.

But as I close the door, I look across the street and get a shock. Pearl's has been bricked.

It's been closed for years and the name, *Pearl's Jewellers*, has nearly faded off the front. I always thought it was a good name for a jewellers, a pity it shut down. Now there's this black hole in the glass of the window.

Then I get another shock. The black hole isn't a black hole at all, but Mrs Pearl herself, in her black coat with a little black hat sitting on her head of black hair, and she's facing her own window with a hand up against the glass.

What's she doing?

Her left hand hangs down by her side, but her right hand is lifted with the fingers spread so her fingertips touch the glass, not pushing hard, it doesn't look like, but just touching gently, her head turned slightly to one side. She looks as though she's listening for something, checking, remembering . . . I don't know. I've never seen anybody concentrate so hard on a dirty shop window. She stands like that for a minute or more and I watch, then suddenly she drops her hand and turns to stare at me.

She's small, not much taller than Matty but a lot thinner, and quite old, seventy or older, and her eyes are jet black, glinting in her wrinkly bird's face. She stares so hard it spooks me out. She's double density, Mrs Pearl, like those black holes in space that suck everything into them. You hardly ever see her out in the street, but when you do, it stays with you for the rest of the day.

I have an idea: I could do Mrs Pearl for the Someone Else's Shoes Project, which takes more explaining than it's worth but here goes.

Every Monday we have PSS – 'Personal and Social Skills' – which involves Mr Ash telling us not to bully, get pregnant or take drugs. We say yeah and then do homework for the rest of the period. At least, that's how it used to work but PSS has just been given to a student teacher who doesn't know what the deal is and she's come up with the Someone Else's Shoes Project – and she's asked us to do some work!

We've got to find an older person ('not a relative') and interview them about what they were doing when they were the same age as us, the purpose being it helps us understand ('empathise with') other people and generally make us better at relationships.

You could see the thought bubbles rising from everybody's head: *No way!* and *We need to explain something here!* Of course there isn't a thought bubble coming out of Eddy Slaphead but his jaw drops.

He says: 'We've done relationships – the three Rs.'

Everyone goes: 'Oooo!'

Eddy plays to his audience: 'Yeah: Rights, Respect, and, er, Revenge.'

'An interesting aspect of a relationship, that last one,' says the teacher.

'No,' says Eddy: 'I've got it wrong, not "revenge", er...'

'Rhubarb!'

'Rhino!'

'Rectum!'

The class has a field day till she can get order again. She's not backing down; she says we've to do it. Well, good luck to her. Me, I think it's easier to just get on with it, no point in arguing.

Mrs Pearl can be my someone else's shoes. Her shoes are black, like everything else she wears. Briefly, I have the thought of slipping them on my own feet, and I shiver.

I'm listening to the voices in the back: Angi and someone, a man. It's a voice I think I've heard before; I realise who it is.

Norman Parks.

I look back over the road but Mrs Pearl's disappeared before I can go and speak to her. I don't want to have to trail all the way across town to interview my nan, which is Plan B, and anyway Mrs Pearl might be interesting. I don't know anything about her. I'll go over this evening and ask if I can interview her.

'Shop!' I shout at the back room. I could have been a customer.

Angi sticks her head round the door.

'Oh, it's only you!' she says.

'Sorry to be a disappointment,' I say.

Norman Parks is hovering behind her.

'What's he want?' I say.

'Ellie, meet Norman,' she says.

'I already have. I asked what he wanted.'

The smiles freeze on both their faces. I don't care.

'Norman's asked me out on Saturday night,' says Angi. 'That's not a problem, is it?'

'Not a problem for me,' I say, ''cause I'm going out too, with Anna. But I don't know what Matty thinks about it.'

Angi gives this brittle little laugh, as if I'm joking. Norman Parks gives me the dead eye. Between us, it's hate at first sight.

5

So what do you think? Who gets to go out Saturday? Me or Angi?

Correct.

I ring Anna up to tell her.

'Me too,' she says. 'I've got to stay in with the twins. Great, isn't it? They go and have children, and then just abandon them. We'll all end up in care. I blame the parents!'

The twins are Anna's stepdad's and they live up in the village where Anna and her mother used to live. I've never met them, even though their dad brings them down sometimes so Anna can babysit. She says they're okay but you wouldn't choose to live with them so she's not sorry they're mostly up in the village.

But staying in's not too bad a deal because Angi says

I can have a video – one for me as well as one for Matty – and I can have a truckload of crisps – anything I want. She's happy; I'm sort-of happy.

I'm even happier after Norman Parks has gone. When he calls for Angi it's obvious he's decided to try a charm-offensive on me, and when that fails he tries it on Matty.

You can divide people into three groups where Matty's concerned: the ones who just can't handle him and avoid him, the ones who are relaxed about him and treat him like they would anyone else, and the other group, the largest, who do their best but are not happy. They put on these fixed smiles and talk to him as if he's a two-year-old. Call me biased but I think Norman Parks is in the first group, a natural Matty-avoider, but because of Angi he's going to try.

Matty's willing enough; he brings over his favourite videos one by one to show Norman Parks, the kerpow-splat videos he's watched so often the picture's all broken up though he still knows exactly where the kerpows and splats are. Norman Parks takes the boxes one by one and tries to be interested, but it's so obvious he's only doing it for our benefit, not Matty's. Angi is getting her stuff together and keeps glancing over at them, and sure enough, he smiles slyly at her and once even winks. He wants me to laugh at the way he's disappearing under these boxes of videos and because it's a joke Matty's not in on, I'm not going to.

They clear off out eventually but we've hardly settled down to watch Matty's video than the kitchen door flies open.

'Da-dah!!' Anna announces herself.

She waves some Bacardi Breezers at me.

'Ellie and Anna's treat. Why should we miss out? Paid for by Brian's guilt money,' she explains.

'What's he guilty about?' I ask.

'Well, being Brian, for a start,' says Anna, then drops it as the twins follow her in. 'I'll tell you later. Meanwhile, meet the gruesome twosome! Diarmid, Declan.'

'Hi!' I say to these lads who stand there waiting for further instructions, but then the one called Diarmid goes over and sits next to Matty.

'What are we watching, then?' he asks Matty.

'Vidyo,' says Matty.

The other one, Declan, hovers, lost. He's wearing a black killer-death-Goth hoody, with the hood up, though I suspect it's the toughest thing about him, more Marilyn than Manson, and he's soon happily munching crisps on the settee with the rest of us. I look along the line of heads – Matty, Diarmid, Declan, Anna – with the nutty-professor light flickering on their faces and feel contented.

'Domestic bliss!' Anna whispers to me. 'Till the rest of them get back. Want another Breezer?'

We go into the kitchen.

'Mum and Brian wanted to go out and "talk about things",' says Anna, and does the quotation marks in the air with her fingers. 'At least Brian did and Mum said okay. She's got more patience than Boltby General Hospital!'

Sometimes Anna's truly inspired. She makes the teachers nervous.

'But I don't know what they're going to talk about. Mum was fed up working from home so she buys the shop, and then she decides we might as well live in the flat over the shop. The idea is we'll see Brian and the twins sometimes – like, how bothered am I about that anyway? So Brian's up in the village on his own and spending most of his time down the pub as per usual, ignoring the twins, not that they'd notice, and I think something happens with a woman from the pub, can't imagine what. Mum finds out and says that's it.'

'Wow!'

'No, Ellie, not wow. You should see the woman, and that makes it worse.'

I say: 'I wish Angi could say: *That's it!* She lets them treat her like dirt and keeps going back for more.'

'If Muzz went with someone else, would it be worse if she was dead gorgeous or barfing ugly?'

'But what's that to me? We're not going out or anything.'

'Okay; so you say, okay. But just supposing, Ellie.'

'But we're not; all right?'

Anna says: 'If she's ugly you think: *So how bad do I look, then?* That'd be terrible. Whereas, if she's gorgeous you can think: *Well, fair enough, and she'll soon move on to someone else, and it'll be his turn to get dumped.*'

'I wouldn't think I'd think either,' I say. 'I'd just feel sad.'

'God, Ellie! Well, that *would* be sad!'

We go back to the settee.

I disappoint Anna is what I feel, I've made the conversation go more serious than she wants, and however hard he tries, Eddy Murphy can't cheer us up. Before the film finishes there's a knock on the back door, and when I go, it's a man I don't recognise.

'The legendary Eleanor!' he says.

'What?' I say.

He's thirty something, forty, and looks sad and cheerful at the same time.

'It's not Brian, is it?' calls Anna. 'Tell him not to bugger about if it is.'

'Such a sweet child!' he says.

'What are you doing back so soon? It's not closing time yet, is it?' Anna asks him as he walks into the back room. They're not like stepfather and stepdaughter at all, more like husband and wife. So this is Brian, father of the twins.

'Don't, Anna!' he says, almost pleading with her. 'I don't need this just now.'

'It's your mess,' she says.

'Okay, okay,' he says, eyes glancing at me, wondering what I know. 'Bacardi Breezers go down all right?'

Anna shrugs. 'A breeze.'

Brian gives up and sits down on the arm of the settee and watches the film with us, occasionally saying something like *Is that the same fella we just saw?* or *Jesus! These special effects – marvellous!* or *Look at that, boys!* We're all willing it to finish. Someone texts Anna to say they're coming round to see her, so she says, and she can't get out of the door fast enough.

'Chuck 'em out soon as it ends, Ellie!' she shouts as she goes.

When they've all gone I put Matty to bed, do a story. He's tired and nodding off before we even finish.

I open the last Bacardi Breezer, take a glug, and it tastes sour and flat. Maybe it's because everybody's gone.

I put in my video, fast forward through the trailers, and start watching, kneeling in front of the telly, and you know how with films as soon as you see the characters and in two seconds you've worked out what kind of people they are, the good guys, the dodgy guys, and in two minutes you know how it's going to end, but that's all right because it's like a really comfortable armchair you can lie back and relax in – well, not this time. It's just too obvious and I can't be bothered.

I rewind the video, and switch the telly off. After the crackle of static, the room is completely quiet.

I know what I have to do. I go into the shop, switch on the light over the writing desk, open up the top, take the minute book out of the drawer, open it.

It hasn't been going too good, my writing career. Last time I opened the minute book, all I did was stare at the blank page, daydreaming, till my eyes went funny. I haven't written anything in it since ~~Daz 15~~.

But now I have something to write about: Mrs Pearl. Now I've been to interview her I can put myself in her black shoes and tell her story.

I turn the page, pick up my pen, and then do what Mr Carmichael suggested: I breathe in. Inspiration.

For a moment I think I've hyperventilated: it's gone completely quiet outside and I feel as though there's nothing outside the little tent of light made by the lamp. No Matty, no Angi, nowhere, nothing.

I begin to write.

6

KRISTALLNACHT

The city was the only place Ruth had lived; she could not imagine why she would ever have to leave, but she did leave, on her own, and never returned.

Vienna was everything a city should be: full of stone buildings and confident citizens. Visitors from the countryside gawped at the well-dressed city-dwellers as they strode through their streets. In the countryside life was hard. Cows were precious enough to have names and were watched closely for signs of illness – a dead cow was worthless. In the city, though, no one seemed to know or care about the existence of cows; milk was something that found its way into the shops and cafés by magic. They took it for granted, like the city itself. It just was.

Like every great city it was built on a river, the Danube, a river famously blue, tons of water waltzing restlessly towards the distant sea.

As well as its river, the city was famous for its music. Composers and musicians had been born here or moved here. There were orchestras, opera houses, bands in the parks, songs in the cafés. People thought the music flooded out of the very stone, unbidden, as if it couldn't help itself, as if the river were making music instead of just being the slopping of cold water. The citizens believed their walking feet couldn't help but dance out the rhythms of waltz and polka on the pavement.

Now, look into a flat in the city, and see a girl practising the piano: Ruth, trying to play a Chopin mazurka. Her mother is putting Ruth's younger brother, Benjamin, to bed in his flannel nightshirt. Downstairs in the jeweller's shop her father is using a magnifying glass to sort diamonds so small they look like granules of spilt sugar.

Something is about to happen.

The city is not happy. The river never runs blue these days; it is a cold slab of grey steel. The citizens on the streets dance no more; their walk is the sore tread of unhappy and overweight people in search of a café and a slice of cake. The only feet that skipped belong to the edgy visitor from the countryside worried about her cow and eagerly looking forward to going home to the village, to the violinist and the accordion player.

The prime minister had been assassinated; a more powerful nation to the north had taken control; gangs

42

would suddenly appear in parts of the city and pick on people, sometimes beating them up. Bloodstains appeared on the pavement, turning brown as the hours and days passed. Graffiti was daubed on walls, warning, threatening, and often it included the black broken cross that Ruth soon learnt was called the swastika.

And yet the city averted its eyes, looked away, as if nothing unusual were happening. Ruth's parents said nothing to her, though sometimes they talked in low voices, lapsing into silence if she came near. It was from friends she found out what was going on: who had been attacked, which family had moved out of the city, which shop had suddenly closed down. It was friends who made it clear that the city no longer loved all its citizens, and it was friends – those who had been friends – who made it clear to Ruth that she and her family were among those who were no longer welcome.

The one who stopped coming to Ruth's flat. A second who didn't walk to school with her any more. The third who didn't send a birthday invitation. Nobody said anything; they just crossed the street if they saw Ruth coming. Only Helmut made a point of coming to the shop in his new Hitler Youth uniform and telling Ruth to her face that he would have nothing more to do with her because of who she was, what she was.

Helmut was a thirteen-year-old kid. It wasn't so long ago that she had made him laugh so hard he had wet himself, and now here he was, made bold by his uniform, telling Ruth and her father that they were a different species from him. He rounded off his announcement with a salute that still needed practice.

'Heil Hitler!' he yelped and went out.

Ruth shrugged at her father as if she didn't care. Fathers had to be protected.

One by one the shops refused to serve Ruth and her mother. In the end only one shop, run by an Italian family, would sell ice cream to Ruth and the two friends she still kept.

And now this night has come when everything is changed, the night that came to be called Kristallnacht.

There's a shout in the street. Ruth stops playing the piano. The shout is too faint to hear the words distinctly, but Ruth knows from the familiar shape of the shout – three syllables with the last one stressed – what it is: Ju-den Raus!

Jews out.

No, she thinks, we're not coming out, we're staying in.

Then she hears another sound: breaking glass. And again. And again. Windows being smashed. From inside the flat it's a small sound, like a wave breaking on a beach, even a delicate sound, like the jingling of chandeliers in one of the dance halls when the heavy-footed citizens waltz to 'The Blue Danube'.

Kristallnacht. Crystal Night. It sounds beautiful if you're not too near, but when it's your own shop window right downstairs it's an ugly, jagged clanging, a bell that tolls the end of the past, the end of Ruth's childhood, and the beginning of a future she couldn't predict.

Ruth runs downstairs and into the shop: her father shouts at her to get back upstairs, but she's so fascinated by the blood that's starting to well up out of a long cut on his forehead he has to push her back up the stairs. He switches off the shop light and stands behind the stair door, holding a handkerchief to his head to staunch the bloodflow, and waiting for the windowbreakers to force their way into the shop. But the shouts die away – Juden Raus! Juden Raus! – as the gang work their way down the street, amazed at how simple it is and wondering why they've not thought to do it before. It's easy to break windows, a celebration, party time!

When it's quiet again, Ruth's father wants to go back into the shop.

'To leave diamonds in a shop with a broken window – madness!' he says.

Ruth's mother opens the stair door, switches on the light and waves an arm at the glittering debris.

'David, nobody else would want to search for diamonds with their brains leaking out. Do it tomorrow. I'll wash that cut and we'll talk about where we go.'

He looks at her, then drops his eyes. She's right; everything has changed. They have to leave.

But after she's washed the blood from his face, he goes back into the shop anyway and starts sifting through the broken glass, looking for the twenty-seven minuscule gems he knows are there. That he will find them, Ruth has no doubt.

Then the second thing happens.

Ruth is gingerly trying to loosen some glass from the window when from the top of the window a long dagger of glass falls free, silent and sudden. It slices through

Ruth's sleeve as easily as it sliced the air, and embeds itself in her arm.

Ruth gives a cry, of surprise rather than pain, drops her arm and the glass falls to the floor. When her father looks at the wound it seems to be only a small cut and hardly bleeds; in fact, the damage is so slight they both think the difficulty Ruth has in moving her arm is only shock. It will wear off, they agree. Ruth is reluctant to add more problems to what the family already face and in the six weeks that pass before she leaves the city her arm is never properly treated.

The glass shard has severed a nerve. For the rest of her life her left arm will dangle by her side, practically useless.

But meanwhile there are lives to be saved, there's a clamour to get aboard the train, the Kindertransport that will take some hundreds of lucky children out of the city and westwards across Europe to the safety of the future.

They decide Benjamin is too young to go with Ruth and will stay with his mother. The rest of the family will leave the city as soon as they hear Ruth is safe and travel to join her by whatever route they can. Because they have a plan, there is no need to worry, and when Ruth is safely stowed on the train at Westbahnhof her excitement and anticipation will be such that she will hardly register what will prove to be the last time her father's beard brushes roughly against her face, her mother's soft and fragrant skin briefly warms her cheek, and her little brother screws up his face to avoid her kiss.

It will be ten years later, in a quiet and orderly embassy room in London, before she learns when and where they died. The man who tells her is a survivor of the camps, a hollow-faced Pole with bad English, who had witnessed so many terrible things he'd decided to treat them all as a big joke. Ruth left as soon as she could, to walk the streets with the tears making her lips salty.

Benjamin would have been nine when he died: was the Fatherland such a delicate thing it was afraid of nine-year-old boys?

But long before that embassy interview, there will be the freezing journey west on the train from Vienna, with the unexplained halts and the equally unexplained starts. Once, after a long wait, they will began to roll back east; the travellers will stare at each other in silence, their hearts in their mouths, till the train stops, then resumes the journey west. They will cross the border into Holland and finally get out when the railway track ends at the North Sea.

They will enjoy the kindness of strangers in Rotterdam and, after a rough sea crossing in a ferry awash with vomit, will arrive in the safety of England, whose language will become Ruth's language, so that her own withers and dies, like her useless arm.

A life Ruth didn't choose herself, but was chosen for her, by Kristallnacht...

7

I stop writing, because I don't know how to end it, because it isn't ended. Ruth is alive and well and living on Victory Street.

When I knocked on Mrs Pearl's back door, she opened it so quickly it gave me a scare, as if she'd been waiting behind the door.

'Um, hello, Mrs Pearl, I'm Ellie.'

'I know,' she said.

She peered out of the shadow and waited for me to do the talking. Already I was wishing I'd invented Someone Else's Shoes like the rest of the class.

'I was wondering if I could come and interview you, sometime, for school. Please.'

'Interview?' she said, frowning. 'What kind of interview?'

'About when you were young,' I said. 'My age.'

Mrs Pearl stared and doesn't speak.

Eddy Slaphead's claimed to have found someone who was a chimney sweeper's boy and got stuck up a chimney on his thirteenth birthday. When he was asked how long ago this was meant to have happened he said: 'In the olden days. Like, this guy went to see the Beatles play live!' Miss, the student teacher, didn't say anything, let it go. She's learning.

'But maybe you can't remember,' I said to Mrs Pearl, for something to say, and immediately realised it must have sounded rude.

She didn't look annoyed though, and instead smiled a slow, thin smile.

'Oh yes, Ellie. I can remember.' Then she said: 'Look after your little brother, Ellie, because no one else will. I know.'

The conversation wasn't making any sense. I'd made a big mistake with Mrs Pearl. If Eddy can invent a chimney sweeper's boy, then I'm sure I can come up with someone, a suffragette who chained herself to the Mayor of Boltby or something.

'I'm sorry,' I said, backing away. 'I shouldn't have bothered you.'

'Come in!' she said. 'You're welcome.'

'Er, right now?'

'Come in!' she demanded, and turned back into the kitchen, leaving the door open and me with no choice but to follow her in.

The kitchen was bare. My nan's house is crammed full

of things she's had since whenever – jars, pots, little pictures, embroideries, her apron, ovengloves, plates on the wall, photo of her wedding, cookery books, recipes on scraps of paper, collection of silver paper, jar of 1 and 2ps – stuff it's taken her a lifetime to collect, and she's been hard at it. But in Mrs Pearl's? One cooker, old but clean, standing on its own. A white pot sink. A cupboard. A table with two chairs. And that was it. It didn't even have that old person smell.

'Sit down, Ellie,' she said, and pointed at one of the chairs. She sees me staring at her bad arm.

'You want to ask me about my arm?' she asked. 'Is that the kind of question you have for me? Well, I'll tell you.'

And she did. I didn't have to ask any questions; Mrs Pearl didn't need to be encouraged. She just talked, about a time and a place I'd never heard of.

She talked about Kristallnacht and a girl called Ruth; herself.

She had a pale face, or maybe it was her eyes being so dark made her skin seem pale, her eyes that fixed me and never wavered, and a mouth that moved constantly, releasing words that didn't have a trace of a foreign accent but that were too perfect for someone born in England, words that built a family, a city, a whole history in front of my eyes.

I've never looked at someone for as long or as hard. I'd never realised how much stuff there is in one small head, that heads are much bigger than the space they take up.

And then, when she'd finished speaking, I had a weird moment. All evening I'd been listening to Mrs Pearl talking about Ruth, as if she was talking about a different person, but now the words stopped and she looked down sadly – and suddenly I saw a girl being told off by her mother for something, a kid who could have been me. Ruth, whose mother would soon be dead in one of the camps.

I couldn't help it, I just filled up.

You know when you cry, someone usually always puts an arm round you? Not Mrs Pearl. She stared across the table at me.

'No point in crying, Ellie. It doesn't do any good. The only thing is to remember what I've told you, and if someone tries to tell you it didn't happen, someone who is old enough to know better, then they are evil, and the only thing to do is to spit in their face and turn on your heel because that person is not fit for this world!'

I wiped my eyes with the back of my hand.

'Have to go,' I mumbled. 'It's late.'

I couldn't get the door open and Mrs Pearl had to do it. Before she let me out she said: 'Look after your little brother, Ellie.'

'Yeah. Thanks.'

And I made a dash for it.

Now I read over what I've written. I feel good because, well, I've written it and it's a million times better than ~~Daz 15~~ and maybe I won't have to go back to Mr Ash and tell him being a writer was just a joke. I wonder what Mrs Pearl would think about it, and whether to show it to her.

8

I can't sleep. It's one o'clock in the morning. It's stuffy in the attic and the binbag's making its crackling, snapping noise, but it's thinking about Ruth that's keeping me awake. I can't get her out of my head.

The Bacardi Breezers have made me thirsty so I go down for a drink of water, checking who's in as I pass along the landing. Matty's fast asleep, doing his snuffly, blocked-up breathing, but Lewis's bed is empty. No surprise there, then.

I pause at Angi's door. Not a sound. I push it open carefully, just in case. The quilt on her bed is undisturbed, so she's not in either. I could be angry if I wanted, but there's no point. I've got used to it. *Look after your little brother because no one else will*. As if I needed telling.

I tiptoe downstairs – if Matty wakes up you've to get into bed with him to comfort him back to sleep – and open the door into the back room.

Angi *is* in. She's asleep on the settee and alongside her, also asleep, is Norman Parks.

He's lying face down, snoring, still wearing his black leather coat and it's spread over Angi's top half. For an instant I think she's wearing nothing at all, then I see it's just that her skirt's rucked up nearly to her waist.

I stare at the two of them, I can't help it. She's still got her knickers on. Maybe they fell asleep before ... but I don't want to think before what.

Norman Parks is a black, leathery, malevolent thing, like a huge bat, one claw hanging onto the floor, the other lying across Angi's legs. She's completely defenceless, but trusts the whole world. Poor Angi, who just gets used again and again and again.

I walk through to the kitchen, take a glass off the shelf as noisily as I can, and run the tap, letting the water drum into the sink. There's stirrings in the back room.

'That you, Ellie?' Angi asks, her voice a bit husky.

I carry the glass of water into the room. She's sitting up and pulling her skirt back down, a bright, strained smile on her face.

'No,' I say, 'it's Ruth.'

She frowns and I go back upstairs.

9

I can hear someone blowing something. It's an ordinary school day, and downstairs someone is playing what sounds like a mouth organ.

It's 8.00 – I've got to sort Matty!

I jump out of bed and do a quick room check: neither Matty or Lewis is in their room, though Lewis's bed's been slept in. I'll say this for him: however late he comes in he still gets up in time to get to work. I look round Angi's door. She's fast asleep – alone. Thank God last Saturday and Norman Parks was a one-off. On the other hand, one-offs isn't what Angi needs.

'Sort Matty, will you, Ellie?' Angi mumbles. She's not asleep, then, just leaving it to me.

The sound of the mouth organ's coming from the shop, from the wardrobe. When I get there and open it up, Matty's sitting inside, blowing and sucking into it, not a tune, just this wheezy in-out, in-out rhythm. He must really think it's party time because he's got the fox stole round his neck, too. He's in his element.

'Where did you get that, then?' I ask.

Either he can't hear me, or he ignores me. He must have found it in a drawer somewhere. God knows who's blown through it before and what terminal diseases they had; it looks disgusting.

'We'll have to get going, Matty. It's time for school.'

He keeps playing. This is going to be difficult.

I hold my hand out to him and shout: 'Come on! Let's get some breakfast.'

I persuade him to come through to the kitchen, though he doesn't stop playing. It's starting to get to me.

'Here!' I tip some frosties into a bowl, pour milk over them. 'Eat them; I'm going to get dressed.'

When I come back down – uniform on, tie done short enough to take the mick, the bit of shadow and liner you can get away with – he hasn't touched his frosties. He's discovered how to move the mouth organ sideways across his lips, very fast, to make runs up and down the scale.

'Come on, Matty,' I plead. 'We've got to go!'

He ignores me. He discovers how to do the sideways thing at the same time as the in-and-out thing. It's starting to *really* get to me.

'Matty!' I yell. 'Eat your fucking frosties!'

He stops playing, blinks at me, then bursts into tears.

'No need for that!' says a voice behind me.

55

It's Angi in the doorway, hardly awake, looking dog rough.

'Now what've you done to him, Ellie?' she asks.

I'm speechless.

'C'mon, Matty, eat your breakfast,' she says.

I say: 'Yes, well, see if *you* can get him to stop playing that thing and eat his frigging breafast.'

'What is it?' asks Angi, peering at the mouth organ in Matty's fist. I think she needs glasses, but she won't admit it. 'Oh, it's a what-d'you-call-it. Go on, Matty, play us a tune!'

And Matty, who's just taken his first mouthful of cereal, ever keen to oblige, blows into it again. It makes a funny gurgling noise and milk drips through it.

Angi laughs.

'Practice makes perfect,' she says which makes me mad because it's the kind of thing stupid people say.

Then she says: 'I've going back to bed, Ellie. I'm not feeling too good. Something I ate.'

Matty holds the mouth organ up, watching the milk drip out of it, then looks at me and grins.

We'll both be late for school, but what the hell.

I grin back at him, after all, it's only a normal day. A bit different maybe; today I'm going to do my Somebody Else's Shoes in PSS – I've got *Kristallnacht* in my bag.

At least that's the plan.

I'm chatting with Anna on the science corridor at morning break when something starts happening down the far end and the deputy head goes flying down the corridor with a couple of heavyweights – you know, the sort of teachers who really wanted to be bouncers. Next thing they're bringing Robert Hearn out, feet first, with blood all over his face and shirt.

'Gang of Pakis jumped him in the toilets,' someone tells us.

'Couldn't have happened to a nicer guy,' Anna mutters to me.

I know what she means. Robert Hearn – 'Hernia' – is a prize pig, racist, sexist, you name it, but Anna knows better than to say it too loud. There's six or seven of us watching Robert Hearn leave a trail of blood on the corridor floor – I notice Muzz behind me. Two or three look at him. He's the only Asian in the group, on the fringe, a bit separated from everyone else. There aren't many Asian kids in the school, mostly they go to St Peter's. Muzz reckons not to notice anything, then he looks up, decisively, and stares at one kid.

'What's up? It's nowt to do with me.'

But the kid keeps staring at him, as if he's saying: *It is something to do with you.* And after a few seconds, Muzz drops his gaze, as if he has to agree. It is something to do with him.

Then someone comes down the corridor with a different version. There wasn't a 'gang', only two Asian lads; they'd only been trying to stop Robert Hearn scrawling racist graffiti on the wall and it was Robert who'd started the fight.

'I didn't know he could write,' says Anna.

But another lad has just been to the toilets and there isn't any graffiti on the wall so *that* version can't be correct, but somebody else claims that the caretaker has just been in to clean up the blood and got rid of the graffiti at the same time. Then somebody *else* says they're all talking about the wrong toilet!

It's obvious everyone's going to believe the version they want. Robert Hearn is taken to Casualty and it's either a nose bleed and he's right as rain, or a fractured skull and he's in intensive care – take your pick.

The bell goes for the next class, which is PSS and I go in thinking I'm going to be telling the story of Mrs Pearl and *Kristallnacht* but Miss has other ideas. She wants the class to discuss Robert Hearn and 'this major incident' before we continue with Someone Else's Shoes.

'I think we can all agree this isn't the kind of thing we want going on in this school,' she says.

Nobody speaks.

'Or any school,' she says.

Peter Swift and his mates, the out-and-out racists, aren't going to risk saying anything. Outside the classroom there's no stopping them, but none of them's going to volunteer now; they know they'll just get bawled out, so they'll keep it for later. It's a lad thing, apart from Rachel Hardy who hates everyone, herself most of all, and wears a permanent scowl.

'Last week Tom told us about someone who fought in the Vietnam War and I think we agreed violence isn't the solution,' Miss says.

Then there's another, bigger group, Eddy Slaphead,

Lisa Kildare, ~~Daz 15~~ people like that, who'll reckon to laugh at the Asian-taxi-driver jokes but you can tell their hearts aren't in it. You know they aren't going to give Miss what she wants.

'So, who's going to start us off?' Miss says.

Rahel Kapoor, the one Asian girl in the room, isn't going to volunteer either, that's for sure. She wouldn't say boo to a goose. She stares at her desk and won't look up. I don't blame her.

'Any suggestions about what we do about the way things, er, flare up here between students?' Miss says.

At last Eddy sticks his hand up.

'You mean, between them and us?' he asks.

'Well, it depends who you mean by "them and us",' says Miss, and I'm wondering what's come over Eddy.

'Obvious who them and us is,' says Eddy, looking round and grinning. 'And obviously it'd be better if they all went to St Peter's, to the Paki school.'

Silence for a second, then the guffawing starts and one or two cheers.

Miss is taken aback, actually steps backwards.

'If you don't mind, without the offensive language.'

'I thought we were to say what we thought about Hernia getting beat up,' says Pete Swift.

'I was inviting a discussion in civilised language,' says Miss. There's a look of panic in her eye.

'You got it wrong, Eddy,' says Pete. 'It's not what she wants to hear. Hey, Miss, if you put your fingers in your ears you won't get upset and we can have the discussion. How about it?'

I'm wishing Anna was in this class. She once took on Mr Taylor in maths, so legend has it, when he was being sarcastic at Eddy's expense. It wasn't even her battle and Eddy was too dim to know he was being sarcasticked at in the first place, but Anna kept going at Mr Taylor till he threw her out of the class. But she's not here now and anyway she wouldn't be defending Eddy if she were. What's happened to him? He's never said anything like that before: *the Paki school*. Has he caught it from the Pete Swifts and Rachel Hardys?

Miss decides to abandon her discussion.

'Okay, class, if we can't discuss it in a useful way let's skip it. We'll carry on with Someone Else's Shoes. Come on, settle down! Okay. Now, whose turn is it?'

Nobody speaks.

'Have you done yours yet, Rachel?' she asks.

'Yeah.'

Miss is desperate for an ally. She spots me and I can see the relief on her face as she remembers it really is my turn.

'Eleanor! If you'd be so kind.'

Everyone looks at me. Time for Mrs Pearl and *Kristallnacht*.

I stand up. There's a bit of smirking and murmuring when I start telling the story of Ruth in Vienna and how her family were persecuted because they were Jews when the Nazis came to power – Pete Swift mutters to his mate and they laugh – but when I tell them about how the shop was smashed up on the Night of the Broken Glass, of the decision to send Ruth away from

Vienna, of the fate of her family in a concentration camp, they all go quiet again, and by the end, they're all riveted. The sun's shining on my face and I keep my voice calm but passionate at the same time and as I tell them the prejudice Ruth suffered in Vienna is the same as Asian people are now suffering I can see it's really getting to them. Pete Swift stares at his desk, Eddy turns and looks up at me, the sun catching his face too, and I can see he regrets what he said about St Peter's being a Paki school. When I finish the mood in the room's changed completely.

I wish.

That's what the film would look like.

To begin with, I don't stand up – nobody stands up in class unless they're ordered to at gunpoint – and when I open my mouth I see Rachel Hardy scowling at me. *Yeah? What you got to say about anything, Eleanor? You and your Victory Street friends?* is what I feel she's thinking. And I can't do it; the minute book stays in my bag; *Kristallnacht* and Ruth never get a mention.

I can't do it.

Instead, when I start speaking what comes out is the story of my American uncle (who I haven't got) who went to a school where they were all ordered to sell chocolate to raise funds for the school and because he refused he was bullied by a gang called the Vigils, and he still refused and in the end he was beaten . . . that's right, it's the story of *The Chocolate War*, the book I've just read, and I'm hoping no one else in the class has. I can't think of anything else and I just want to get through.

Miss is watching me and I don't know if it's because she's read *The Chocolate War* too but she looks disappointed. I think she wanted me to come out and say something about the Robert Hearn incident, something on her side. She doesn't know how hard that would be.

I finish. Some more people do their Shoes. The game now seems to be to make it obvious the accounts are total porkies but it's not even funny any more. As Miss listens to them her eyes go completely dead; she knows she's lost and the class has won, but of course the class doesn't feel good about winning. We can't get out of the room fast enough when the lunchtime bell goes, and leave Miss standing there looking as if she'd like to commit suicide, or murder.

On the corridor I go straight for Eddy.

'What's happened to you, Eddy? Had a brain transplant?'

'You what?'

'Signed up with Hernia and Pete and them, have you?'

He turns to face me.

'I haven't signed up with nobody.'

'It didn't look like it. I couldn't believe it was you talking.Tell me it wasn't you talking, it was Pete Swift throwing his voice.'

'I don't need anyone to do my talking for me, Ellie. If you can't see the problem in Boltby, well, that's your problem.'

'What problem, Eddy, what problem?' I'm nearly shouting I'm so exasperated, and what makes me more exasperated is I know what he's going to say.'

62

'Asians, of course, that problem.'

'Rahel Kapoor, she's a problem?'

''Course not, her.'

'Or Muzz?'

'Not provided he dun't get interested in my sister.'

'So why would that be a problem, Eddy?'

He laughs as if it's so obvious he doesn't need to say.

I say: 'So what else is he banned from doing? Going in the shops – except for the Italian ice cream shop of course.'

Eddy looks even more puzzled than usual.

'Sorry, Ellie, but I've got to go. Dinner dinner dinner dinner...' he sings it like the Batman theme. It's an old joke and neither of us even smiles. I watch him go.

Oh Eddy! I used to love you for your stupidity and now I hate you for it.

'You'll get run over if you stand there!'

It's Mr Carmichael behind me.

'You look fed up, Ellie. Anything I can do?'

I shake my head.

'Any inspiration recently?' He's remembered! 'Or just perspiration?'

I think of the minute book in my bag, of Ruth missing her chance in PSS, and I think: why not?

'Actually, Sir, yes, as it happens. Want to have a read?'

He doesn't blink. 'Of course.'

'By chance,' I say, opening up my bag and getting it out, 'I just happen to have it with me.'

I hold the book with its blue binding and gold lettering towards him. It feels odd: the book that should

63

live in the drawer in my writing desk is now in the wrong place, exposed to school smells and school sounds. I glance round, hoping no one's watching, and wondering if I'm doing the wrong thing.

He takes it and opens it.

'No!' I say. 'Don't read it here, Sir, it's private.'

He looks up.

'You sure you want me to read it, Ellie?'

'Yeah, okay, but not here.'

He shuts the book, puts it under his arm, gives me a close look.

'You okay, Ellie?'

'Yeah.'

'Things all right at home?'

'I suppose.'

I used to tell him about home and he'd try to talk me up. Once he lent me *Matilda*, laughing as he gave it me: 'If you think you've got it hard, Ellie, wait till you read about her parents!' I appreciated him making the effort and it was a great book, but fiction is fiction, isn't it?

He wants to help now, so I have to give him something.

'Sir, d'you think Matty will be able to come here?'

'How old is he now?'

'Ten. His birthday's in November.'

'Hmm,' he says, and looks at his feet. 'Of course, it's not up to me, but why not?'

Then he says: 'To be honest, Ellie, it wasn't easy for the last Down's syndrome kid who came here. They had to take her away in the end, put her in a special school.'

'Poor kid.'

'I don't know. Perhaps she was better off there. You wouldn't believe it but she got picked on here.'

'The kid who picks on Matty is dead!' I say. *Look after your little brother*.

Mr Carmichael laughs.

'But you wouldn't be around all the time, Ellie!'

'I'll know,' I say.

'Maybe he'll be fine. Anyway, I've got to go; important documents to read!' And he waves the minute book.

I say: 'The first bit's nothing really, just a list of people. It's the story about *Kristallnacht* I want you to read, Sir.'

'*Kristallnacht*, eh?' he says, making it sound more German and less mysterious. It was a new word for me and now it comes home that it's a word that other people know, not just Mrs Pearl. 'I'll read it now, Ellie, come to the staffroom when you've had your lunch.'

And he goes off with the minute book.

The staffroom's an amazing place, all those teachers together in one room. One at a time, they're okay, just a teacher at the front of the class, but get them all together and it's like a trip to the zoo, all these exotic creatures herded together. And, as it's lunch time, it's a trip to the zoo at feeding time. Mr Stanton chews with his mouth open and a lump of something stuck on his beard, Mr Davies has dribbled down his front, Miss Rogers eats her yoghurt delicately, dead classy, with a plastic spoon, and a new teacher guards his lunch box like a trainspotter. A couple of them glare at me; they obviously think I shouldn't be in here. They're right.

I try to concentrate on what Mr Carmichael is saying but it's difficult. We're trapped in these low seats where you either have to lean back, as Mr Carmichael does, or perch on the front edge, like I do, to stop Mr Davies staring up my skirt. They're the kind of seats we can't give away in the shop.

'It's very good, Ellie,' he's saying. 'Very confidently done.'

'Thanks, Sir.'

'Yes, very good indeed. If you were any of my other students I'd ask where you got it from.'

'What?!' I'm scandalised he can even think it.

'I said *if* you were.'

I say: 'I suppose I did get it from somewhere. It's a story from someone where I live, from Victory Street.'

'Inspiration, eh, Ellie? Out of the air?'

I say, 'Mrs Pearl's kitchen.'

'What does she think of it?'

'She hasn't seen it.'

'But isn't the story hers? I mean, I know it didn't write itself, but all the same, it'd only be courtesy, Ellie.'

'Yeah, I suppose. But I don't like giving my book away. It felt funny today, giving it to you, Sir. It's special.'

Mr Carmichael laughs.

'The temperamental artist! Hows about I photocopy it for you; would that help?'

'Okay, thanks, Sir.'

He goes over to the photocopier in the corner.

Two teachers are talking about the Robert Hearn incident.

'What's that?' Mr Stanton asks, turning towards them. He hasn't heard about it.

'A fight in the toilets, Phil,' he's told – and you know teachers must have first names but all the same, you wish you didn't actually have to hear them. 'Looks like it's racist.'

'No surprises there,' said Mr Stanton.

'One boy's been taken to hospital.'

Mr Stanton shakes his head. 'One of ours or one of theirs?'

I can't believe he's said it.

'Robert Hearn. One of nobody's, I'd say!' says the other teacher and laughs, but no one else says anything. Maybe they're used to it. Maybe they didn't hear. Maybe. Then I remember I didn't say anything back in PSS, waited till after the class to speak to Eddy, and for an instant I'm so angry with myself and with everybody in the room that I open my mouth to say something to Mr Stanton. I can hear gentle sounds: the shush of someone reading a newspaper; the rustle as someone works through a pile of marking; Mr Ash speaking quietly to Miss Conrad; the photocopier humming as it lights Mr Carmichael's face from below – and I can't do it. If I speak my voice will cut through the soft sounds of the room like a blade slicing a bus seat. I'll be the one being awkward, making trouble.

The moment passes. I look at my knees, hating myself.

'Here you are, Ellie.'

Mr Carmichael's shoes appear in front of me, those old-fashioned ones with a pattern of little holes in them.

He's not sitting down. It's time for me to go.

'Thanks, Mr Carmichael,' I say as I take the book back. 'Oh, I meant to ask: what is a "minute" book anyway?'

'For writing minutes in,' he says. 'When you have meetings and you need a record of what's said, well, the secretary or somebody writes it down and that's called the minutes of the meeting.'

'Why?'

'Well, you might want to check what was decided at the meeting.'

'No, I mean, why are they called "minutes"?'

'Good question; I don't know. And when you've sat through the meetings I have, Ellie, staff meetings and suchlike, "hours" would be more like it. Days. Weeks!'

'Just wondered, Sir,' I say. 'It seems like a funny word.'

'Yes,' he says. 'Funny beasts, words.'

10

Muzz is looking grim.

'Yeah, I know,' I say, 'all that Robert Hearn stuff.'

'You what?' he says. 'I'm not thinking about that. Muzz's got bigger problems. Like, his grandad has found him – from Pakistan, thank you very much! – a fiancée!'

He says 'fiancée' really French.

'You're joking, Muzz!'

'Sounds like a joke, does it, Ellie? If I wanted to tell you a joke, I'd tell you a real one, like: knock knock.'

'Sorry, Muzz.'

'Come on, do it right. Knock knock.'

I sigh. 'Who's there?'

'Bushra, Pakistani bride, looking for Muzz.'

'That's not a joke,' I say.

He looks glum. 'I know.'

'Is that what she's called?' I ask. 'Bushra?'

'How did you guess?'

'You're hard work today, Muzz.'

'So'd you be if you'd been told you had to get married.'

'I suppose you can say no.'

'Yeah, I can – and be black sheep of the family. Asian sheep. They'll never speak to me again.' He pretends to perk up. 'Hey, now there's an idea!'

He goes glum again, then pulls a photograph out of his pocket, passes it to me. It's a girl formally posed in a photographer's studio in front of an artificial background that's meant to look like an English garden with a painted fence and gate, and painted roses.

She is beautiful, absolutely gorgeous, except... she can't be more than twelve, thirteen tops.

'Bushra,' announces Muzz. 'My fiancée. Maybe.'

'But when's this going to happen?' I ask. 'She's well younger than me.'

'Old photo, and anyway, after twenty years of serious chapatti-eating she'll be as fat as me mum's friends.'

'Muzz,' I say and poke him in the ribs. 'You're just a sexist pig!'

He puts on his Pakistani accent: 'You should be knowing it is insult to call Muslim a pig.' Back to Lancashire. 'Not like your mum, though, she won't get fat. Anyway, what happened today at school that was such a big deal?'

'You know, with Hernia getting beaten up,' I say.

'I didn't know you cared about him.'

'Of course I don't care about him; that's not what I'm talking about.'

'So why was it a big deal?'

'Well, I'm not talking about me specially. Miss thought it was a big deal, she tried to get us to talk about it in PSS. Like, oh yeah!'

It's a peace offering but he doesn't want it.

'What does she know?' says Muzz: 'Robert Hearn gets what's coming to him and the whole school has to know about it, discussions in PSS, and that. Brilliant! Fucking brilliant! What does Miss know? What do any of you know?'

'Muzz!'

'No big discussions about Kali, were there?'

'I don't know. And who's Kali?'

'Exactly!'

'Exactly what?'

'Exactly you don't even know who he is. Goes to your school, sorry, *our* school, and you don't know who he is.'

I'm getting just a teeny bit fed up here.

'Maybe I do,' I say. 'He's a bit podgy?'

'Seen him, have you? Well, he's quiet, he's Indian so he's really on his own, keeps his head down. A few weeks back he goes to the toilet, same famous toilet as today, Hernia and his mates are in there, waiting, not for Kali in particular, he just happens to be the lucky one. It's the end of the lunch break and Hernia's been stuffing his face, you know, pizza, double chips, I don't know,

71

beans, triple beans, he's bursting! They get Kali's bag off him, he's not going to fight, is he? Hernia takes the bag into a cubicle while his mates keep hold of Kali, make sure he doesn't say anything. After a bit, Hernia comes out of the cubicle, gives Kali his bag back, tells him to go and keep his mouth shut or else. Kali shoots off, can't understand why he's got off so lightly. Then he starts to think he can smell something, something disgusting, and looks in his bag. And guess what he finds, Ellie?'

'You're joking!'

'You keep telling me I'm joking, Ellie. I should go in for stand-up! Here's one I heard the other day. What do you call a Pakistani on the moon?'

'Oh, Muzzy!'

'Go on: what do you call a Pakistani on the moon?'

'Don't know.'

'*A problem*. What do you call *all* the Pakistanis on the moon? *The solution*. Good, innit? If it had been "the final solution" it would have been a real killer!'

He's so bitter there's nothing I can say.

''Course there's no PSS discussions about Kali,' Muzz says quietly. 'Nobody knows about it except me, and I only found out because I'm in the same Maths group as Kali and that afternoon he had to reckon he'd forgotten to bring in his homework and no way was I going to believe that! Kali's does his homework before it's even set! Afterwards I got him to talk, told me what happened. You know what, Ellie, what really got to me? He felt ashamed. Hearn sticks his fat arse in Kali's bag

72

and shits on his books, and *Kali* feels ashamed, as if it was what he deserved, what he was worth. He didn't want to tell me, and if he knew I'd told you, I don't know, he'd probably kill himself.'

I shake my head. Muzz is right: I don't know the half of it.

'Yeah, not Hearn, he doesn't feel shame, he feels great, the amazing arseman! Turds R Us! It's Kali what wants to crawl off and die.'

He goes quiet, then looks at me.

'Ellie, why don't you have nothing to do with me at school?'

I'm shocked.

'Muzz, I'm sorry about Kali and everything, but you're going to have to back off a bit. How d'you mean, I don't have anything to do with you at school?'

'We're talking now, but you don't at school.'

'Muzz; I don't not talk to you at school.'

'"Don't *not* talk to me". Hang on, let me work that one out. "Don't not".'

He mimes 'deep thinking', puts his fingers to his chin and narrows his eyes.

'Isn't that a double negative?' he says. 'Does it make a positive though? Like two blacks don't make a white. However hard they try.'

'Muzz! Stop this!'

'You don't not talk to Mr Carmichael, but in fact you *do* talk to him.'

No secrets in Northend High, that's for sure.

I say, 'At school we're either in lessons – remember?

73

– or we're going to lessons, so when's all this talking meant to happen?'

'It's okay,' he says, suddenly very sad and quiet. 'It's just you get tired of getting knocked back. You try, best behaviour, like you've swallowed the book of etiquette, and it doesn't make no difference. This white kid you thought was fine, suddenly they've backed off. I can't blame them; they only need to say 'Hiya' and their mates are calling them a Paki-lover.'

'Dun't bother me!' I say. 'I'd rather be a lover than a hater!'

And without thinking whether anyone's watching or whether Muzz would take it the wrong way, right there, in the middle of Victory Street, I give Muzz a big hug and kiss him right on the cake-hole.

He grins, and waves the photograph of Bushra at me.

'You'll have to join the queue, mate, with all the other Paki-lovers. I'm having to fight them off!'

11

It's a couple of days later and I've picked Matty up from school. We're walking up Victory Street when we see a youngish guy coming towards us, eyeing me up. Matty pulls in close to me, so I have to hold him off to maintain my poise.

The guy passes us, doesn't say a word.

'Huggy!' whispers Matty.

'You what?'

'Huggy!'

Well, I can't give Matty a hug and look cool so I ignore it. Matty's stopped walking and he's staring back at the guy; he's not happy about something. While we watch, the guy sticks something on a lamppost, very deftly, glances round, then walks on.

'What's he doing?' I say. 'Let's go and look.'

Matty doesn't want to, so I go back on my own.

It's a sticker, some racist rubbish. I skim it quickly:

Knights of St George
RIGHTS FOR WHITES
Are you sick of being last in the queue
while 'ethnic minorities' and 'asylum seekers'
get free housing and full benefits, ect.
Don't be a foreigner in your own country!
Phone ...

It's part of what's happening: the skinheads in the red car, Taj's uncle's shopwindow, Eddy in PSS, and now racist stickers going up, all in this area. Doing it just to provoke, perhaps, to get Taj to do something stupid? Not difficult.

We go home, pushing the copy of *Kristallnacht* through Mrs Pearl's letterbox first. I hope she likes it, but you never know.

Lewis is in the kitchen.

'What're you doing home?' I ask, surprised.

'What do I do with these?' he says by way of reply, holding up some frozen beefburgers.

'Boil them,' I say.

'Yeah?'

''Course not, you useless get!' I'm laughing, it's meant to be a joke but Lewis seem to have forgotten how to laugh. 'Fry them, or do them under the grill. It's not exactly *haute cuisine*.'

'*Haute cuisine*!' he mimics, then scowls and sticks them under the grill, four of them.

'You doing one for me and Matty?' I ask.

'Didn't know you were coming home.'

'Yeah, well, it's really unusual for us to come home after school!'

'How am I meant to know? I'm only here now because we finished early, power cut at work.'

'Well, it's nice to see you! Say hello to your big brother, Matty. Remember him?'

But Matty's found his mouth organ and can't even hear me. I persuade him to sit outside on the shop step so the rest of the street can get the benefit.

'Mangi's gone for some bread,' says Lewis. 'She asked if you could stop in with Matty tonight.'

'No danger of you doing, I suppose?'

He snorts and doesn't bother replying.

'True love, is it?' I ask.

'What?'

'Angi and Norman Parks.'

Lewis laughs. 'Might be for Mangi; not for him.'

'Yeah,' I say sadly. 'It always is for her. Anyway, how come you know what Norman Parks feels for Angi?'

'"Feels" is the word,' says Lewis and makes a dirty groping gesture with his fingers. Then he says, a bit shiftily: 'Guesswork, little sister. And Mangi's past form.'

That's a throw-back to before, 'little sister', when Lewis was my big brother who could do no wrong. We were like that: big brother, little sister. But now I think he's just mocking me. Something changed when he left school and started work. I don't really know what he's up to any more and when we meet, we don't speak, not really.

'Nah,' he says. 'I'm not stopping in. Who'd want to stop in in this house, shop full of junk, complete mess. Like living with the Addams family or something.'

I feel a sudden flare of anger. Lewis is never in so it all gets left to me. He doesn't even pay rent.

'Feel free to help out any time you want!' I say.

'Nah, it's okay. Keep well away, I say,' he says. 'Mother a fucking nymphomaniac—'

'Lewis!'

'Sister very friendly with the boy next door, *very* friendly. Except the boy next door is . . .'

He pauses, looks at me.

'The boy next door,' I say, 'is Muzz.'

'Yeah. Muzz. And as for little brother, well . . .'

He laughs and looks towards the shop, where Matty's giving the mouth organ plenty.

'Well,' he says, 'we all know about little brother.'

My mouth's hanging open.

'So, nah, I'm not stopping in. And with a bit of luck, little sister, I should be fixed up with a flat soon.'

All I can think to say is: 'Them beefburgers are burning.'

He glances at the blue smoke billowing up from the grill.

'Ah, fuck 'em. I'm off out.'

He walks straight out of the door.

I've stopped crying and thrown the beefburgers away by the time Angi comes in with a couple of loaves, and she's in busy-busy mode, looking forward to tonight, so she doesn't even notice anything's up.

There's nothing to tell her, nothing that would help. It's

Ellie's problem.

But it's not all bad: Anna rings and says her mum and Brian are going out for, in Anna's words, another mega-session of staring up their arses, so since she's on guard duty for the twins, do I want to come round with Matty, bugger homework?

It's an offer I can't refuse, and it's even attractive enough for Matty to leave his mouth organ at home. No mouth organ, bliss!

Anna and her mother have a totally different set-up from us, livingwise. For a start, they don't live in the back of their shop at all but above it, in a flat. Anna says her mother used to do hairdressing in their front room; when they got the shop she was adamant that work would be kept downstairs, upstairs was for living, 'if you can call this living,' says Anna.

That means their lounge is upstairs, which is a bit weird and wonderful, looking down on what's going on in the street and the people not knowing. It also means they don't suffer from the problem of *Angi's Antiques*, which is furniture crawling out of the shop and into the back room. And it means *their* furniture looks as if it's been actually chosen; it has a bit of class.

Their vase has flowers in it unlike ours which has some rubber bands, the card for the video shop and biros that don't work. Their videocardrubberbandbrokenbiro holder is a pot that Anna made and which she says is just too amateurish but her mother insists on keeping. Angi wouldn't even know I'd made a pot, never mind want to keep it. ('But I love your house,' says Anna, 'it feels like nobody gives a damn!' Which I could find pretty hurtful given she knows it's me that tries to keep it tidy.)

'Hi,' says Anna as she lets us in. 'They're out already, so we can trash the joint!' And seeing my expression adds: 'Joking, Ellie. The twins'll do it for us.'

Tonight I need to talk about Lewis, but only if she's in the mood.

The twins are sitting on the settee watching the box. Matty plonks himself down in the middle, and I follow Anna to her bedroom. She wants to show me a new top. She puts in on.

'Yeah,' I say. 'Great. Fine.'

'Nah,' she says, taking it off. 'A big mistake. I just wanted confirmation.'

'But I said it was great!'

'It's not what you say, it's the way that you say it. Is that a song title?' she says. 'Here; you try it!'

So I put it on and it fits pretty good.

'Yesss!' says Anna. 'That's the one! You fill it out better than yours truly, the titless wonder. You should go down a storm with the lads next Saturday.'

'Next Saturday?'

'We never did get our night out, remember?'

I can tell tonight's not the night to talk about Lewis.

Declan and Diarmid haven't moved since we left them. Matty's doing his best, talking them through his brum-brum, but not getting much out of them. He stops trying to get a response and pushes it around on the cushion, brum-brumming quietly.

'Okay,' I say, switching off the telly. 'Story time!'

'Hey!' say the twins together, and Anna looks at me askance.

'Story time? I don't think the twins do that one, Ellie.'

'What do they do, apart from TV?'

No one speaks, then Anna says: 'Go on, boys, show Auntie Ellie you've got a story in you.'

They keep silent, stare at me.

'Right!' I say. 'We need some characters.'

'What's a character?' asks Declan.

'Like a person, Declan, except not real,' explains Anna.

'Not real?' he repeats. 'Like Connor and Christy?'

'Who?' I ask.

Anna rolls her eyes. 'One of Brian's stupid ideas.'

'We don't know if it's a stupid idea, do we?' says Diarmid. 'Your trouble is you think you know everything, Anna.'

'But what *is* the idea?' I ask. 'Who are ... what were they called?'

'Christy and Connor, our great-great grandfathers,' says Declan. 'No! Great-great-*great* grandfathers.'

Diarmid sees I'm completely mystified and grins at me. 'What it is, is Dad says our ancestors came from Ireland, ages ago, twins called Christy and Connor, and in Ireland in those days the only thing to eat was potatoes, but the potatoes got this disease so everybody starved. Brian says millions of people died of hunger or left Ireland. Some came to England, like Christy and Connor, and others went to America.'

'I didn't know about any of this,' I say.

Anna says: 'Brian does, and don't get him started on it

or you'll get the wide-screen, dolby-wrap-around-sound version. I think it's just one of Brian's yarns. It only takes a drink and he's off!'

'I believe it,' says Diarmid simply. 'Why not?'

'Why not because nobody can have *two* great-great whatever-it-is grandfathers with the same great-great grandmother, a simple matter of biology, neh!' And she does that sticking her tongue behind her bottom lip thing.

Diarmid looks a bit hurt so I come in: 'So he didn't want to give you the same names, in memory sort-of-thing?'

'Dad says it would've been bad luck,' he says.

Anna adds: 'Plus which it's traditional to work through the whole alphabet in twos: Christy and Connor, Declan and Diarmid, Edwin and Egbert, Fergus and Fastfood, Groby and . . . '

'Okay, Anna!' says Diarmid. I'm getting to like this kid who stands up to her; there's not many who can, and that includes me.

I say: 'So we've got two characters. Matty, who's yours?'

'Chrackatous!' says Matty.

'Yes, have you got one?'

'Chrackatous monster.'

'Matty's favourite, the monster,' I say. 'Okay, Matty, what's he called this time?'

Without hesitation Matty says: 'Huggy.'

'Sounds a very friendly monster,' says Anna.

'Nah,' says Matty. 'Snot friendly. Huggy.'

And hugs himself hard.

Then it clicks.

'That guy you were telling me about, Anna, the one who

squeezed Matty. That's who he is, this "Huggy".'

'Who was?' says Anna. 'I know I told you about – yeah – but who you on about now?'

Then immediately something else clicks, or semi-clicks, if you can have a semi-click.

'I'll be back in a minute,' I say, jumping up. 'Got to check something.'

I'm down the stairs and out on the pavement faster than Matty can come up with a second chrackatous. I get the wrong lamppost first time, but then I see it. The Knights of St George sticker.

Someone's been trying to scratch it off and it makes it difficult to read, but I can make out the drawing clearly enough: St George killing the dragon. Why didn't I register it the first time?

Norman Parks. His trademark.

I pick up a stone and start rubbing at what's left of the sticker.

'You don't get rid of it that easily!' says a voice behind me.

I spin round. A small woman, old, in black. Mrs Pearl.

'I think it's coming off,' I say, carrying on scratching at it. 'Nobody can read it now.'

She watches me for a moment, then says: 'The bloodstains on the pavement didn't turn brown, you know. You got that wrong. They weren't left there long enough.'

I stop scratching. She's read my *Kristallnacht* story.

'Too much you got wrong!' she says, angrily. 'We must talk again. Come on!'

I follow her across the street to her house.

12

'The bloodstains on the pavement didn't turn brown. I
didn't say that. Why did you write it, Ellie? The blood
wasn't left there long enough. In the mornings they
would make us scrub it off – not myself, you
understand, it wasn't the children they forced to clean
the pavement but the adults. They enjoyed humiliating
the men especially, getting them to do the work of
maids, and the older the men, the better. And by the
time the people walked to the café for their morning
coffee and slice of strudel there wasn't a mark to be
seen.'

I'm back in Mrs Pearl's clean, sparse kitchen,
sitting at the same table, the same clock ticking on the
wall. I'm not sure if she's angry with me or with what
happened all those years ago.

'You said people were killed on the streets, Mrs Pearl. I assumed . . .'

'Don't assume, Eleanor. You thought it would be nice to let those red stains slowly turn brown, like autumn leaves or something, little dabs of colour, as if you were painting a picture. People like nice pictures so that's what you did. You painted a nice picture.'

'I didn't know a detail like that mattered so much,' I say.

I'm feeling a bit hacked off because, well, I sat at this table for a whole evening listening to her telling me stuff that could have been an invention for all I knew and I did my best with it – and now she's telling me it wasn't good enough! But if she can tell what I'm feeling, it doesn't make any difference to her. She fixes me with her black eyes and I have to stare back. It's like looking through the skylight into the night, without the glimmer of a star.

She's in full flow again.

'Sometimes there was nothing on the pavement, no blood at all, it was perfectly clean, but they would still make three or four old men, respected elders with their long beards and long black gaberdines, get down on their knees and scrub at nothing.

'Once they made Jews cut the grass in the park, with scissors. They ordered the whole park to be trimmed, but after laughing for an hour at the line of grandfathers slowly cropping the grass like black sheep, they got bored with the joke. Nobody would believe it now, but I saw my mother tend the blisters on Grosspapa Schreiber's fingers

85

caused by that morning's unaccustomed scissor-work. Do you believe it, Eleanor?'

'Why not?' I say.

'Why not? Because it was only a detail, my mother puncturing the blisters so the fluid ran out over his old hands, and they are both dead, my mother, old Schreiber, for half a century, so you only have the word of a mad old woman living on Victory Street.'

'I don't think you're mad,' I say.

'The other children do; they keep away. I wanted a house like my grandmother's, always people coming and going, laughing and arguing, that kind of house, but no, that's not what happened. Here, nobody calls. Will you call again, Eleanor?'

'Of course!' I say, trying to mean it, but already she's back in Vienna.

'Sometimes they used scissors on the men; their long beards were too inviting. It only took two Brownshirts to hold somebody's grandfather so he couldn't move while a third – snip snip! – clipped his beard off, and if they snipped a piece of ear off too, well, that didn't matter provided they didn't get blood on their uniforms.

'You know, Ellie, they were so obsessed with being smart, with cleanness – cleanliness. Wash, scrub, trim, tidy: oh, everything so orderly, so neat. But underneath, was filth! They were filthy! They were destroyers, haters, murderers!'

Her eyes blink, as if there's something in her past that even she can't look at, and the next thing tells me what it is.

'You know, I could have brought Benjy with me on the train to England. There were other children as young. I should have brought him with me.'

Mrs Pearl smiles a sad smile at me.

'Excuse my temper, Ellie; so you get a detail wrong, sixty years ago? It doesn't matter. Your *Kristallnacht* is good, except for the ending; you want it to be happy. What was it you wrote? "The safety of England". Well, after Vienna it was, yes, but it wasn't really little Ruth welcomed with open arms by England, Mr Churchill coming down to meet me off the ferry in person with a bag of sweets. No, we were treated as nuisances, pests, just as asylum seekers are treated today. There were the same Jew-haters in Britain as in the rest of Europe. My husband – the man who was to become my husband – was put in a camp in the Isle of Man as an "enemy alien", as if he was from outer space, just because he was German. But in Germany David Pearl had worked day and night *against* the Nazis!'

I need to get away from this woman whose stare is so piercing I'm beginning to know how a kebab feels. I'm meant to be having a laugh round at Anna's!

'Ellie, you like my piano?'

I look round the room. No piano.

'Where is it?'

'In a flat in Vienna, where a young girl played Mozart, not so much Chopin, by the way. Where did you get the mazurkas from?'

The drawer of my writing desk, that's where, but no point in telling Mrs Pearl that. Another wrong detail.

'Pianist was going to be my career. But a one-armed pianist? No. Better a jeweller with Mr Pearl in Boltby – except the town became poorer and poorer as the years passed, and the shop bell didn't ring so much. Then David died and I was stranded here, with nowhere to go.'

She shrugs, as if such things, the things that happened to her later on, were not so important.

'It's time to let you go, Ellie: I shouldn't have kidnapped you. But one last thing I must show you, one last detail.'

She reaches down, takes off her shoe and puts it on the table. What on earth is she doing? She puts her hand into it and pulls out a little twist of ancient-looking paper.

'You didn't put this in your story – didn't I tell you about it?'

She opens it expertly, with her one hand. In the wrinkles of the piece of paper there's a little sprinkle of salt or sugar, glittering.

No, not salt or sugar.

'I carried this little package all the way to England, here, in my shoe. My father gave it to me when I left. Not just diamonds, Ellie; these are called "brilliants", perfect cut diamonds, the best. Crystals from Kristallnacht. It was my insurance policy, if times got hard. And times did get hard but how could I ever sell them, my father's last gift? And do you know what "gift" means in German?'

'I had to do French at school,' I say.

'It means "poison", that's what; in German "gift"

88

means "poison"! At the end of the war, the British parachuted parcels of food and clothing down to the defeated Germans. The parcels were all labelled "gift", they couldn't understand why the Germans weren't grateful! I thought my father was perfect, Ellie. I thought he was God. But he died in a concentration camp. And there are only twenty-four stones here; he couldn't find the last three among the broken glass!'

Mrs Pearl laughs and lets me out onto the dark street. I can breathe again.

13

Anna goes ape when I get back, and I'm still so taken over with Mrs Pearl's story and the sound of her voice, that I can't even think what Anna's problem is.

'"I just got to check something," you say, "back in a minute", and that's it: you disappear! I follow you down after a couple of minutes. No sign. Go round to your house. Completely dark. Come back up here. No sign. Go down again. I think: she's been abducted, definitely. Good, I think. And it turns out you've bumped into Mrs Pearl and gone back to hers. Well, that's great, really great! My turn now, is it? Abandon the kids and go and find a pensioner to have a cup of tea with?'

'I didn't have a cup of tea.'

'Why not? You had long enough; you could have got her life story.'

I think: well, there *is* a reply to that, but now's not the time. I'm starting to go off Anna; if everything doesn't go just as she wants, forget it. In fact, I'm starting to feel she's another one to add to the collection of people Ellie has to look after.

'Anyway, what happened in the story we were doing?' I ask.

Nobody says anything. The boys are back to watching TV.

I try again. 'Huggy monster? The Irish twins?'

'Oh, them!' says Anna. 'They all got binned.'

It takes a long time to bring her round, in fact, it's got to Matty's bedtime before she starts to thaw. I suspect it's *because* it's Matty's bedtime and time for us to go that she starts to chat, just to see if she can switch me on again.

But it's good to have her back, so I update her on Mrs Pearl's story even if it is going to make Matty late for bed.

She listens pretty well for Anna, doesn't say much except for: 'Cutting grass with scissors? I can't believe that!' just as Mrs Pearl predicted, and: 'Sent to the Isle of Man? As if!'

When I finish she says: 'So, happy now, you've got the complete version?'

'Not happy; it's sad, really.'

'And there's someone like that living on your door-step!' She shakes her head, smiling. 'Mrs Pearl.'

I say: 'It's funny: we call it "a story" even when it's true.'

'Except the grass cutting.'

'Oh, that's true, I'm sure,' I say.

'Ellie, she could be a loon, care in the community!'

'Of course she isn't!'

'You're totally sold on her, aren't you? How do you know she isn't making it up?'

'Why would she?'

'False Memory Syndrome?'

'Come again?'

'You've heard of False Memory Syndrome, where some people remember things but it turns out they haven't really happened; they just *think* they remember them. Vivid imaginations or something.'

'But why would she do that?'

'I don't know, banged her head: total insomnia, it's always happening in films.'

'You mean amnesia.'

'Whatever. Or she put a spell on you; she's a pretty spooky kind of person.'

'Anna, for Chrissake!'

'Slipped something in that cup of tea, made you forget.'

'But I didn't have a cup of tea!'

'You only think you didn't because of what she slipped in it.'

'Anna, it's you that's the bloody loon!'

And we're laughing so hard the three boys stare at us. Maybe I'm not going off her.

14

I'm walking down to the town centre.

To get into town you go along Victory Street as far as the corner shop and then turn down Waterloo Road, which takes you to the dual carriageway and straight into town. Waterloo Road humps over the canal bridge and from there you can look round 360 degrees, taking in Boltby and the moors all round it. On a day like today you could almost think the town's safe in the palm of a hand, except you'd have to imagine the hand was wearing a sort of purpley-brown smudgy glove, to get the colour of the moors, and they don't make gloves like that. There's a windfarm on the moors to the south and the sun is glinting on the arms of the windmills as they turn. To the north side the hills are all cool and distant and mysterious; the sun doesn't go there and I don't imagine I will either.

But here the sun is shining, I'm walking into town, and for once, I'm on my own.

Matty is with his dad; Angi's waiting for Imran to bring over some new stuff for the shop; Lewis is I don't know where; Anna is helping in her mother's shop; Muzz has to go to Birmingham to meet Bushra's relatives.

Sunny. Saturday. Solitary.

Total bliss.

There's a gang of pigeons on a roof making smug, gurgling noises, and with the sun warming the roof, I can see how they feel. All at once, just for the hell of it, they take off and I watch them fly, clattering round in a big circle. And, just for the hell of it, I decide to leave the road and cut down the steps to the canal path. It's a longer way round but I'm less likely to meet anyone I know. Prolong the moment.

It's interesting, the canal, watching the changes.

There's another supermarket trolley in the water, keeping company with the one that's been there for months. The kids must go to a lot of trouble to dump them here – it's a long way from the supermarket. You've got to admire them, real dedication.

Some people have made little gardens by the canal: some rose bushes, a miniature lawn no bigger than a snooker table, a few hens pecking a square of soil bare. And one man has got grand plans: he's building a boat. Okay, he hasn't finished it yet – in fact it looks exactly the same as last time I walked this way – but at least it's a plan. Most people have given up on plans and for them the canal side is just a place to dump rubbish: some old window frames, a washing machine, a settee. Waste from the factory has stained the canal bank orange, but not far away some ducks are bobbing up and down so it can't be too toxic.

Across from where I'm walking now there's a factory with a tall chimney, and growing out of the top of the chimney, a small tree. It's daft, like a feather in its cap.

I love it all.

I don't want to build a boat and sail away. This town is where I've always lived, and I love the whole mess of it. Anna can't wait to get out, move to Manchester, hit the city. Me, I can't think why it should be better anywhere else.

The ducks aren't playing, I can see now, but fighting. Three males seem to be attacking one female, in fact, it looks like gang rape.

I throw a stone to break them up, but they scoot a few yards and carry on. Not much I can do about it.

I walk on, prolonging the moment, but I won't be able to make it last for ever.

I'm going to see Norman Parks.

I'm going to tell him to stop seeing Angi and I know that's mad, pointless, but I can't stand how things are, how she is.

He never comes into the house now, which is fine by me, and instead sends one of his taxis, *sends* one, he doesn't drive it himself, so we get a St George's taxi pulling up in front of the shop at more or less the arranged time and tooting for Angi. I couldn't believe it the first time.

I said: 'Make him get out and knock!'

But Angi said brightly: 'Oh, it's all right, Ellie, I'm ready anyway.'

Though she wasn't really and goes to the door to wave a just-a-minute finger at him. I'd have given him the fingers for two-minutes.

Once the taxi toots so late – Angi prowling about and doing annoyed huffing and puffing for my benefit – I think Norman's forgotten about it, and once it doesn't come at all.

And when she comes home, Angi's not good: drunk-miserable instead of drunk-happy, and sometimes so late I don't even hear her come in.

Last week she came in when me and Matty were having Saturday breakfast. We looked round as the key rattled in the back door and there she was: high heels, ankle bracelet, black leather skirt, off-the shoulder top, big dangly earings, tired smile. She'd looked good the night before, but standing there in the morning sun with milk deliveries rattling in the backstreet, no, she didn't look good. I wouldn't want to say what she looked like.

''Lo, Mum!' said Matty cheerfully.

'Hi, kids!' said Angi. 'Sorry, Ellie; I crashed out. Everything all right?'

She sat down and took off her shoes.

'My feet are killing me . . .' and she bent over and rubbed her foot, but I knew what she'd stopped herself from saying: she'd walked all the way from Norman Parks', no taxi had brought her home. I supposed she'd left him snoring in bed.

So I'm going to tell him to leave her alone, find someone else to screw, to screw up.

As I walk by the canal the land to each side falls away and soon I'm looking down at streets and cars. Here the canal is carried over the town on an aqueduct – GOURANGA written on its side – and I leave the towpath and go down the stone steps onto the street.

It's busy, people in a hurry, shoppers, and it's a bit of magic, being able to suddenly appear among them: one minute I'm on my own on the canal bank and the next I'm in the middle of click-clacking sharp-dressers – well, wannabe sharp-dressers. It's like slipping sideways into a different dimension. And for my next trick!

My next trick is to find St George's Taxis and I'm not looking forward to this but...

I go into the first taxi firm I find.

'I'm looking for St George's Taxis.'

'Where you want to go, love?' says the guy.

'I don't want to go nowhere. I just want to find St George's Taxis.'

'This firm is much cheaper.'

'I'm sure.'

'Ask anyone.'

'Look, I don't want a taxi, I just need to find that taxi firm.'

'Okay, I take you there. Free.'

'Is it far?' I ask.

'Not really, end of High Street.'

'I'll walk. Thanks.'

'What you want them for anyway?'

'Oh, personal stuff, you know. Thanks.'

There's several taxi firms at the far end of the High Street and mostly they're Asian, but sure enough, one of them's St George's Taxis. Two cabs are parked outside; they've started flying little St George's flags on the front of their cars.

I walk past and glance in. There's nobody waiting inside; with the holidays starting it's not busy. Norman Parks must be in the room at the back, behind the hatch.

I take a deep breath, walk back, go in and straight over to the hatch.

'Hi!' says the guy behind the hatch.

It's not Norman Parks, it's Huggy, a big St George's flag on the wall behind him.

'You want a cab?'

I breathe deeply.

'I don't want anything from you!' I say.

'Oooo!' he goes, like he's Graham Norton. 'Listen to her!'

He's talking to someone I can't see, right under the window, and whoever it is half stands up and looks round at me.

It's Lewis.

'What're you doing, Ellie?' he asks.

He was preparing to be amused, but I've wiped the smile off his face. He's annoyed.

'I've come to see Norman Parks.'

'To see Norman?' says Huggy behind him. 'That's nice!'

'Shut it, Scott!' says Lewis. 'What the fuck d'you want to see Norman for, Ellie?'

Lewis isn't annoyed; he's furious.

'Do you know this lady?' asks Scott, mock-polite. I'm glad I don't have to think of him as 'Huggy' any more; it was much too friendly a nickname.

'My bloody sister,' says Lewis. 'Half-sister.'

'I think,' says Scott, 'I think I've seen her before. Is that right? Have I seen you somewhere before?'

'If *I* have, I've forgotten it,' I say.

'But there you go, I *do* remember it. Good memory, me. Live in Boltby, do you?'

I don't say anything. He carries on eyeing me up.

'Yeah? There you are then, that's where I've seen you. It's a small world. Aren't you going to introduce us then, Lewis?'

'Scott, don't encourage her, I want shut,' says Lewis. 'Go on, Ellie, fuck off!'

'Where's Norman Parks?' I ask.

'I'm still waiting for that introduction,' says Scott. 'I'll tell you what, Lewis: you set us up, like you did Norman and Mangi, and I'll see you right.'

My head's spinning. I came here to warn Norman Parks off and instead discover Lewis is right in there with them. But what really freaks me is hearing that ratbag Scott using Lewis's stupid nickname for Angi.

If I had a weapon in my hands now, I'd use it. Then I see there *is* a weapon, a mug of coffee on the ledge inside the window.

'Ever had coffee all over you?' I say.

'Temper, temper!' says a voice behind me.

Norman Parks.

'Hi, Eleanor! Long time no see.'

He shuts the door and comes over to me, smiling. Leather coat as usual. He's got a bacon butty in one hand.

'Nice of you to call in and see me.'

I say: 'Leave Angi alone, you!'

'Your mother?' he acts surprised. 'The lovely Angi?'

'She's . . . she's not well.'

'Not well? I'm sorry to hear that.'

'You know what I mean.'

'I'm sorry but I don't, Eleanor. I haven't seen her for, oh, must be a week now.'

'Why didn't she say?'

'Search me, sweetheart; I'd've thought, you know, mother, daughter, no secrets. But like I say, I haven't shagged her for a week. Poor Angi! She must be missing me. But . . . ' And he comes up really close, licking the grease off his lips: '. . . maybe her daughter's ready for it now.'

I push his face away as hard as I can.

He steps back and I flinch; I think he's going to hit me, but he doesn't.

He says: 'Right, you! Don't come in here causing trouble, upsetting my staff. Don't waste time defending the long lost honour of your mother, *long* lost, and don't think you're anything special, either. In fact, you little bitch, don't come in here again!'

He holds his arm out, butty in hand, gesturing towards the door.

'Norman...' protests Lewis behind me.

But I'm out through the door, I'm not staying for any more.

I'd intended staying downtown for a while, look in some shops, go to a café, enjoy doing nothing, but I don't feel like it any more. I might meet somebody and I feel even less like meeting someone than I did before. Stupid Ellie; it went about as badly as it could.

Going back, along the road this time, I'm not looking up at the windfarm, the roofs, the tree on the chimney – I'm staring at the pavement.

Litter, chewing gum, dog shit; but I know enough about clean pavements to prefer them like this. I wouldn't want Norman Parks and Scott in charge of the clean-up; they'd have Muzz's grandad down on his knees faster that he can sell you a mango.

When I get back Angi and Imran are moving some stuff; there's a chest of drawers hanging out of the boot of Imran's car. Declan and Diarmid are sitting in the doorway looking glum.

'Hi, boys!'

No response.

'Don't you want to go off and play somewhere?' Like, you do, don't you?

'Ellie!' shouts Angi. 'The twins' dad asked if we'd keep an eye on them for a bit; can you find something for them to do?'

'Oh, right.'

Then she laughs about how Imran is trying to get a cupboard into the shop: 'You daft twit, Immy! It'll have to be this end first, it won't go the other way.'

She's full of it, so's Imran, and that makes me smile, in spite of how I feel.

'Carry on partying, boys!' I say, stepping over Declan and Diarmid and into the shop.

'They're having the time of their lives,' I shout to Angi. 'I wouldn't want to spoil it for them.'

But Angi's got the giggles and doesn't hear. It's *her* I don't want to spoil it for, so I'm not going to say anything about my visit to Norman Parks.

15

Brian comes back to collect the twins just when Matty is being dropped off by *his* dad – it feels like a child exchange service or something – so they say hello. I can see that Matty's dad thinks Brian is Angi's new boyfriend and almost shakes his head in despair at her rate of turnover. He doesn't stay. I could have explained who Brian really was, but I've done enough on the Angi's-boyfriends front today.

But Brian doesn't seem in a hurry to go and when he says he's been to see his gran in hospital that's my cue to find out more about Christy and Connor and the Irish connection. As Anna predicted, he didn't need any encouragement to talk.

'Glad you're interested, girl,' he says, 'because there's plenty would benefit from finding out what happened to Ireland all those years ago. 'Course it wasn't me gran who was Irish but me gramp, everything I know about the Famine came from him, though it's twenty year and more since he died and he was a senile owd divil who liked a drink and got confused, like I said, and of course he was born in Boltby like me gran, it was *his* grandfather who was born in Ireland and came over to escape the Famine.'

This isn't going to be easy.

'So was that Christy who left Ireland?' I ask.

'That's right!' he says.

'Or Connor?'

'Well, him too!'

I'm beginning to see why Anna runs out of patience with Brian.

'Both of them?'

'They both came over to England, that's right.'

'But they can't both be your grandfather's grandfather!'

'I'll get to that in my own time, girl!' he says.

Angi and Imran come in from the shop, a bit out of breath from moving things around. She's definitely got a thing for Imran, the way her eyes follow him round. She never was any good at that treat-them-mean, keep-them-keen stuff, but Imran's face gives nothing away. Where Muzz is basically a Boltby teenager, Imran is more like his grandad: watchful, doesn't take anything on trust.

Of course I'm worried what Lewis'll do if he finds out, but like I say, from now on Angi's boyfriends are none of my business.

104

'Okay,' Imran says. 'Better go; I'm driving tonight.'

'Thanks, Immy,' Angi says, smiling at him.

Imran smiles at me and shakes Brian's hand – that Asian-man thing – before he goes.

'Want to stay for tea?' Angi asks Brian. She's suddenly got a burst of confidence: let's entertain! And we're talking beans and chips here, damn the expense!

'I wouldn't want to put you out,' says Brian.

'No trouble!' says Angi, and she's off into the kitchen, radio on, singing along, ever hopeful.

I give it another go. 'So when was it, the Famine?'

'The 1840s it was,' says Brian. 'It went on for five years and more, people thinking the harvest was going to be fine, but when they dug the potatoes out of the ground they were already turning rotten. People even boiled grass to make soup, can you believe that? But it didn't do no good, and the British they never lifted a finger to help.'

'The British?' I ask. 'What had it got to do with them?'

'What had it got to . . . ? Because Ireland was part of the British Empire, for God's sake! What do they learn you in school?'

'Well, I didn't know!'

'We didn't want to be part of the British Empire, of course, and later Ireland got independent, but at the time of the Famine we were stuck with it. Two choices there were: starve to death or emigrate, to England or somewhere else. If the famine had been here in Lancashire, the British government would have done something but there was a stretch of sea between England and Ireland so they could ignore us.'

'Didn't the media report it?'

'Media? What, like "we have breaking news from County Galway" and live pictures, do you think?'

'I know there wasn't TV then!'

'There wasn't even photographs, just drawings, and cartoons, that's what they printed in the newspapers: Irishmen made to look like monkeys, cunning scally-wags scrounging off the poor British. So when they arrived in Liverpool, poor and desperate, what kind of welcome d'you think they got?'

He doesn't expect an answer. We sit in silence for a minute, silence apart from Angi singing out of tune.

I say: 'So the twins went to Liverpool?'

'Just passed through, from what I can tell, on their way here. Gramp thought their plan was to go to America but they never left Boltby again.'

'So, what happened?'

'Eleanor, I can only tell you what he told me. The two boys worked in one of the new mills that were being built – Boltby was booming in those days – and then they went and fell in love with a local girl, the both of them. Her family didn't like her being friendly with Irish boys and they took revenge. Within a year all three of them were dead.'

'God!'

'Terrible times they were, Eleanor.'

'And they were killed by the girl's family?'

'We don't know exactly. There's a story in the family that one of the twins was tried and hanged for murder.'

'Wow!'

'I like to think he was defending the girl. That's if the whole thing happened at all.'

'What was she called, the girl?'

'No idea. Everything we know, the whole story, comes from the cousin who reared the baby.'

'Baby? What baby?'

'Didn't I tell you?'

I could scream! Mrs Pearl knew every detail of her story; she would have known how many buttons there were on her brother's coat when she said goodbye on the station, what the buttons were made of, whether they were fastened or not, but trying to follow Brian is like searching the house for one of Angi's earrings: it's in there somewhere, but lost in all the junk.

'No,' I say, 'you didn't tell me about a baby.'

'The girl got pregnant – I suppose you do all about *that* in school, if you don't do history! She died soon after, maybe in childbirth. And that baby was my gramp's gramp.'

'So who was the father?'

But I know the answer as soon as I ask it.

'We don't know; it could be either twin, or even someone else completely. We just don't know, Eleanor. And the cousin who raised the baby was an old tale-teller who liked a drink.'

Angi shouts from the kitchen: 'Tea's ready. Give the kids a shout, Ellie.'

I go to the foot of the stairs and yell.

I know already that I'll have to write it, the story of the twins: it's another story about someone coming to live on Victory Street from another country, like Mrs Pearl. And all right, it's not the twins themselves but their ancestors, a few generations back, and Diarmid and Declan might not exactly live here but it feels like they do as they clump downstairs with Matty.

'Thanks for telling me about it all,' I say to Brian. 'It's dead interesting.'

And immediately think 'dead interesting' isn't the best way to describe a story with murder in it, so for something else to say I go: 'I suppose it's so long ago it's difficult to be sure about any of the details.'

Which makes it sound as though I don't believe any of it and it's all a fairy tale, so I shut up.

He follows me into the kitchen and we all collect our plates. Angi's making a real effort; she's opened a new jar of pickled onions.

We watch TV together, our plates on our knees, our knives and forks clacking as we eat. A pickled onion scoots off Brian's plate and flies across the room which cracks Matty up.

It's starting to feel like they've moved in for good when out of the blue Angi says: 'What's on at the pictures? Why don't we all go?'

Now, normally I'm not going to turn down a film, but we're a big gang and with Angi being a bit hyper it will all be too much, so I bail out, let the five of them go. She'll have to watch Matty; he's getting a bit hyper too.

When they've gone I mooch around for a while: take the dirty plates into the kitchen, go to the loo, do mirror-mirror-on-the-wall.

I'm putting it off.

I switch off the TV and go into the shop, open up the writing desk and fiddle with things in the little drawers above the green leather writing square again: the pebbles, paper clips, the bobbin with the scarlet thread. There are two drawers that I couldn't open before, and this time, when I yank the brass ring, one of them opens with a rattle. Inside there's a handle made of dark wood, and when I pick it up I discover it's an old knife with the blade folded back. Yikes! Colonel Mustard in the library! But the blade is too stiff for me to open, so I put it back and shut the drawers.

I'm still putting it off.

I take out the minute book; it falls open at *Kristallnacht*. That story's fine: Mrs Pearl organised it for me. I turn to the next clean page.

It's me who's going to have to organise Brian's story. I pick up my pen.

16

THE TWIN BROTHERS

There were once twin brothers who lived in the middle of a great island. Their mother had died and they were poor, but as long as the potatoes grew in their small field they were content.

Then one summer a strange blight came to the island. The potatoes rotted in the ground.

The twins starved, every day growing thinner. The father stared at the fire in dejected silence while the twins foraged outside for something to eat.

A man with a cart came by, selling tickets for the ship to Amorica.

'What's Amorica?' asked Connor.

'The land of love,' said Christy who was an hour

older than his brother and knew such things. 'And if we had the money we would go there.'

The next day a dark smiling stranger came to the cottage. He carried a sack.

He said: 'I can lend you the money to sail away. In return.'

Connor said: 'In return for what?'

Christy said: 'It doesn't matter what. We don't want anything from him!'

'Suit yourself!' said the stranger. 'Au revoir.' And he went and waited under the tree at the end of the field.

'What does "O voir" mean?' asked Connor.

'It means "Till we meet again",' said Christy.

That evening the father died. He had just breathed his last when the door opened and the stranger walked in. He bundled the father into his sack.

'We will surely die!' said Connor.

'Yes,' said the stranger. 'You surely will.'

'All right,' said Christy. 'Lend us the money for the ship to Amorica.'

'I will only lend you five sovereigns,' said the stranger who drove a hard bargain. 'Enough to take you to Angerland, not Amorica.'

'And what do you want in return?' asked Christy.

'An "au revoir",' said the stranger.

'Done!' said Christy, and the stranger gave them the five sovereigns.

The man returned with the cart. It was now crowded with children, thin as spectres.

'Room for two,' he said.

Christy and Connor handed him the five sovereigns and climbed up onto the cart.

The stranger was on the roof of the cottage, tumbling it down.

'What do you say?' he called to the twins.

'Thanks!' they shouted back.

'I didn't ask for thanks,' he called, kicking a hole in the roof. 'I asked for an "au revoir".'

'O voir!' they shouted, too excited to care.

The twins travelled a long journey, by cart, by ship, by canal barge, to reach a town too busy to care if people were starving on the island. There were no low cottages in fields here, but cobbled streets and houses with an upstairs, factories with three upstairs, mill chimneys impossibly high. In the mills cotton looms worked their jaws from dawn to dusk, greedy for bales of cotton to turn into cloth, greedy for people to work them.

Connor and Christy only needed their cousin-once-removed to give them a bed, which they shared head-to-toe, and they were ready to be put to work on the looms.

But this was Angerland, and though the townspeople didn't care if the twins had been starving on the island, they cared very much if they came to live and work in the town.

The twins, being trusting boys, didn't see the hatred the town felt for them. They were young and keen and wanted to save the money to take them to Amorica, though the songs they sang at night were full of yearning for the island they had left.

Connor and Christy worked four weaving looms. With

four eyes between them, the twins could keep an eye on each loom and make sure there were no faults. The cloth that flowed onto the four rolls at the back of their four looms was without flaw, pure as cream.

At night they sang their songs and counted their savings, which slowly grew as time and work turned the boys into men.

On the same floor of the factory, a brother and sister worked four looms. The sister was called Dora, which means 'gift'. The brother was called William, which doesn't mean anything.

Their cloth was not faultless. It was full of flaws.

The reason for this was simple. One of Dora's eyes was sometimes watching Connor, and the other was sometimes watching Christy. This wouldn't have mattered if William had made up for his sister's inattention, but he didn't. One of William's eyes was watching the eye that watched Connor and the other was watching the eye that watched Christy, so it was not surprising that William and Dora's cloth was full of flaws and juddered out of their looms like sack-cloth.

William said to Dora: 'Sister, stop looking at the O'Voir twins. They are Irish and are not the kind of people we should be friendly with. Your attention should be on me and our looms.'

Dora said: 'Brother, I will look at the O'Voirs if I wish. They have a beauty that seems to have passed you by.'

William, who was indeed as ugly as a rat that has been flattened with the shovel, said: 'At least watch our looms!'

Dora said: 'It is a mean-spirited person who would sooner look at a machine with the palsy than at human forms such as the O'Voirs.'

William, defeated, said: 'I will tell Father.'

It was bound to happen that even someone as young and innocent as Connor was going to be distracted by the girl across the aisle.

Christy said: 'Connor! Our looms are our passage to Amorica; we must watch them.'

But even as he said it, Christy knew they were lost to the beauty of Dora. He was an hour older and he himself had already begun to return her glances.

William told his father, as he had threatened. His father said: 'The O'Voirs and their kind are the scum of the earth. I will speak to Dora when she gets home tonight.'

But Dora did not go home that night. She walked by the canal with Connor who told her of his love and of his desire to build a boat to sail with her to Amorica.

She kissed him and said: 'Yes, my love, but for tonight let us lie in your bed; that is enough for now.'

And that is what they did, and they did not go head-to-toe.

When Dora didn't appear at home, William's father summoned his four brothers to his table. In the centre lay his knife, with the blade opened.

He said to them: 'Dora has had her head turned by this charmer, Connor O'Voir. I do not have to tell you the land of his origin. I do not have to tell you what we now must do.'

114

Without a word, William's father and his four brothers left the table and searched the streets for Connor.

But the person they found was Christy, who of course was the spit of his brother, and who tonight was walking the streets as there was no room in the bed for him.

The four brothers fell on Christy and held him as Dora's father plunged his knife into the youth's heart.

'O'Voir!' they spat at the body and left it on the pavement.

A stranger came out of a dark alleyway and bundled the dead Christy into his sack.

'That's one!' he said.

In the morning William said to Dora: 'You won't be seeing Connor O'Voir again!'

This puzzled Dora for across the aisle was Connor, as plain as a bobbin, working his looms. William, of course, believed it to be Christy. But Dora said nothing, as it would make life simpler if her family believed Connor to be dead.

Connor hadn't time to glance across the aisle, as he was twice as busy. He knew something was wrong when a scarlet thread appeared in his cloth, running down the middle like a cut in white skin.

He reported his brother missing to the constabulary, but they said: 'Where is the body? Angerland is a just country; don't bother us with your lies!'

Dora told her father she was going to have a baby.

Her father said: 'In that case, since no one else will have you, see if the remaining brother, the left O'Voir, *will marry you. And then, daughter, I will have nothing more to do with you.'*

And that is how Dora and Connor married, and that should have been the end and happily ever after.

But when the baby was born, Dora took one look at it and said to Connor: 'I'm sorry, Connor, but I can see the child's father is Christy. I confess I was in the bed with him first, and not head-to-toe. Forgive me. I loved you both.'

Which, when Connor heard, he was not surprised by; after all, Christy was an hour older than he.

But being unsurprised is not the same as forgiving.

He took the baby boy from Dora and handed it to the cousin-once-removed. Then he took Dora in his arms and hugged her, tighter and tighter, till she died.

The judge said: 'Expect no mercy, Connor O'Voir. You shall be hanged. Angerland is a land of justice.'

Connor was hanged in the town square in front of a silent crowd. A stranger quietly made his way through the onlookers and cut down the body. He stuffed it in his sack, saying gleefully: 'And that makes two!'

And the cousin-once-removed was left holding the baby…

The phone rings.

'*Who's that?*'

'Ellie.'

'*Right, you!*' It's Lewis.

'Oh, hi!' I say.

'*Never mind "hi",*' he says. '*What the fuck did you*

116

think you were doing today, coming down to Norman's, eh?'

'Angi's not good; he wasn't doing her any good.'

'When was she ever good, Mangi?'

'Lewis! Don't call her that!'

'Whatever. Only reason I'm ringing is to tell you never, never do that again!'

I don't say anything.

'Get that?'

'Wasn't thinking of doing it again, Lewis, why'd I want to meet Norman Parks again?'

'He's a good mate, Norm. Says pass my test and I can drive for him.'

'You learning to drive then, Lew?' We don't know what he's up to any more since he moved into his flat; he hasn't even told us where the flat is, never mind invited us over. 'Lessons are dead expensive, aren't they?'

'Lessons? Who needs lessons?'

'I thought – oh, what do I know! You coming round to see us sometime, Lew, tell us what you're doing? Burn a hamburger or two?' I say, risking a joke.

There's a pause. He's said what he wanted but he doesn't hang up.

'You still there?' I ask.

'Yeah, but I got to go.'

'What're you doing with people like that, Lewis?'

'Don't start!'

'They're just stirring things up.'

'They don't need to, with twats like Taj doing it for them. That guy's a complete pillock.'

117

'So? Just because Taj is, it doesn't mean you can have a go at all the Asians!'

'*Don't try to defend him.*'

'I'm not. That mate of yours, Scott, he's a pillock but you don't write off all the whites, do you?'

'*Leave him out of it.*'

'Just making the point: some people are okay, and others are a waste of space, and some's white and some's Asian, and that's all you can say!'

'*Well, you've said enough; I'm going.*'

'You helping them do stickering and that, Lewis?'

Brrrrrrrrrrrrrrrr . . .

I go back to the writing desk and read over what I've written.

And the cousin-once-removed was left holding the baby. . .

And again I don't know how to end it. That's the problem: I want an ending and things don't end.

The cousin-once-removed cared for the baby and it grew up as strong as the diet of poor weavers allowed them to be in those days. And the boy whose name was, oh, could have been Edwin, fell in love with a girl who lived in the town and they had a baby, let's call him Fergus, the first of a houseful of babies, and before you know it they have Brian, and then, hey presto! Declan and Diarmid, alive and well and living their lives in Victory Street. Actually, right now, watching *Men in Black Part Three* or whatever it is.

Mrs Pearl on Victory Street sixty years on, with a stash of diamonds worth a small fortune. She could cash them in and build a community centre and we'd all live happily ever after.

Happy ending.

I put down my pen. I'm going to bed, I'm tired. Angi can put Matty to bed when she gets in; that'll be a nice twist.

17

Taj has a gun.

Nobody knows where the rumour starts and nobody knows why he'd want one. Muzz says there's a turf war breaking out over drugs and I suppose there could be – what would I know about that? Me, I just think it's a rumour started by Taj himself to go with the image, Tony Taj Soprano and all that. Someone's even graffitied the canal bridge on Waterloo Street in big letters: BOLTBY BRONX.

'Is it true, man?' asks Muzz.

'What's that?' says Taj.

He's sitting in the black car, gracing us with a face-to-face interview. And speaking of faces, Taj's is now a real work of art: each sideburn is now carefully carved into *two* parallel lines so neat they might have been done with a ruler and a black felt tip.

'You know what they're saying,' says Muzz.

'Muzzy, you're talking riddles, innit,' says Taj. He's a good-looking guy and he knows how to make people beg. Come on, Muzz, you're worth two of him.

Muzz says, 'Okay, man, suit yourself.'

And immediately Taj laughs. 'Just having you on. Here.'

He opens his jacket up just enough for us to catch a peep of a black metallic object gleaming in the dark under his arm.

'Hey!' says Muzz.

'Just remember, Muzzy, keep on my side!' says Taj.

The car squeals off and Muzz's grandad has to make a dash for the pavement.

'It could've been a hairdrier,' I say.

'Yeah,' says Muzz. 'Dry his armpits with.'

'After he's shaved them so they look like works of art, Picassos.'

'Picasso's whats?'

We laugh, then fall silent.

'One of those replicas, it could've been,' says Muzz.

'Yeah.'

But we're thinking the same thing. It really is a gun, and it's one more thing on the road to wherever Boltby's going, and we're going faster towards it.

I went to see my nan last week, my dad's mum. It's at the other end of town in the middle of a row of terraced houses, and my nan's lived there all her life; it can't hardly have changed in fifty years. It was my refuge

121

when I was little and Angi and Dad were splitting up, and I still get the same feeling when I go into the kitchen and see everything in the place it should be. It's like climbing into my nan's lap, like I used to, and cushioning my head on her bosom, thumb in mouth, while we watched 'Blind Date' together. It's harder now I can't do that and we have to do everything by talking, but I stay an hour or more and everything's fine, though I notice she's got a bit shaky when she makes some tea.

But when I'm leaving I see what has changed; not Nan's house, but all the others. Most of the other side of the street is boarded up, metal sheets over the doorways and windows, and when I look, Nan's side of the street is the same.

'What's going on?' I ask her. 'All these empty houses.'

'It's been going on for a bit, shows how long it is since you visited your nan. Maybe there's been more of them just recent.'

'But what's happening?'

'Council buying them up cheap, want to knock them down.'

'Knock them down!' I couldn't be more horrified if she'd told me there'd been a bombing raid.

'I'm not leaving in a hurry, nor's Billy.'

She points across the street at a house that's looking a bit run-down but has a window box with some flowers; it's the only splash of colour in a street of grey metal sheets. Billy making an effort. For the first time I notice a stone in the middle house with the name of the street carved in it: *Blenheim Terrace 1895*. There's a twiddly

122

line looping from the capital 'B' to the 'T'. proclaiming the confidence of the stonemason who carved it a century ago.

Below it, on the metal sheet over the door someone's graffitied PAKIS OUT. No twiddly bits there.

'But it's getting hard, Ellie, living round here. There's some folk, don't know who they are, come and go in that bottom house. It must be dark inside with the windows blocked off.'

I say goodbye and walk down the boarded-up street, past the crackhouse at the bottom, the once-proud street in which Nan and Billy are the only survivors. If one of Norman Parks' leaflets came through the door, Nan'd bin it, but how about Billy? Maybe he'd believe the rubbish blaming everything on Asians.

I head for the bus station. It's going to be another hot day. Already men have appeared sitting on walls and doorsteps, stripped to their shorts, one or two with a can of beer, watching me as I walk past. I pass more lamp-posts with Knights of St George stickers.

At least I think she'd bin it.

18

I asked Brian where the graves of Connor and Christy
were and he said he thought they were here, but now we
can't find them.

We're in the graveyard of a little chapel right out on
the edge of town, half way up the moorside and right
below the windfarm. Each windmill is like a two-bladed
propeller and they sigh slightly as they turn. You're
aware of them all the time, these giant personages like
those big heads on Easter Island all facing the same way,
looking over our shoulder.

'Don't look now,' says Anna, 'but I think we're being
watched.'

Anna was a bit sniffy about coming at all.

'You want to look round a *graveyard*, with *Brian*,' she
said. 'Well, I suppose they go together.'

'Only Brian knows where it is,' I said.

'I suppose.'

Diarmid says he wants to come too, to see his great-great-great grandpa's grave.

On the way up Brian said: 'At least, I think this is the right place.'

'You think!' cried Anna.

'It's my da told me about it – or was it my ma? I've never been myself.'

'Diarmid,' said Anna, 'prepare for disappointment. You may never meet your descendants.'

'Ancestors, you mean,' Diarmid said: 'Descendants is the future.'

'Got something planned, have you?' she asked.

The chapel is abandoned and on the way to being a ruin. The windows have long since been smashed and there's a gaping hole in the roof. Two black rooks perch on the little bell tower and caw at us; they seem glad to see some visitors.

We stoop over the weathered gravestones, working our way along the rows. Some are broken or fallen, some are impossible to read. The gravestones are old enough – some go back in the 1700s and we're looking for one around the 1850s – but we can't find one for Christy McManus. Then Brian has a thought: it's his grand*mother* who is descended from Christy, and he's damned if he can remember what her maiden name was, but was it Donnelly?

Then he has another thought: the cousin-once-removed gave the baby *her* last name, and was that O'Brien?

By now Anna and Diarmid just take the mick, putting on these terrible Irish accents.

'Bejesus, would it be a Doyle she'd be, me grandmother?'

'Holy mother of God, but I think you've got the wrong generation there; it was a Donovan she'd be after being, or do I mean Doolan.'

I think O'Voir stands as good a chance as any other of being the right name.

Then Brian delivers the killer punch.

''Course; Connor's not going to be here. A convicted murderer's not allowed to be buried in consecrated ground.'

'What's "consecrated" mean?' asks Diarmid.

'Holy,' says Brian. 'Blessed by a bishop.'

'But this is abandoned; it won't be holy now.'

'It was then, when these were planted.'

Then he says: 'Or maybe it's the one who's murdered who's not allowed in. '

It's hopeless; we're not going to find it. I can see why Anna runs out of patience with him.

We give up the search and lie in a row in the afternoon sun, the four of us. We must look comical to the rooks, lying there in the graveyard, waiting to be planted, as Brian puts it. Behind us the giant propellers turn slowly, sighing.

'Jesus, I wish they'd turn them up to full blast,' says Brian. 'Make a bit more wind to cool us down.'

I'm starting to wish I hadn't put Christy and Connor's story in the minutes. Brian's just a joker; you can't trust a word he says.

19

Anna's meeting me to go shopping. She's late but it doesn't matter; I sit by the bandstand and watch the skateboarders. They're pretty hopeless. As it's early afternoon the shoppers are still looking energetic and hopeful and because of the heat nobody's wearing much. You could almost believe the town is at ease with itself.

'Eyeing up skateboarders? I don't think so!' says Anna when she arrives.

'Have to do something while I'm killing time.'

'Crisis in the tint department – I had to run to Asda for exactly the shade of vomit some old crow demands.'

We walk towards the clothes shops; we've promised ourselves we'll both have something new for the weekend.

Someone wolfwhistles, which is nice of course but you can't look.

'How you doing, girls?' someone calls. The voice sounds familiar.

I shoot a quick glance to my left, and see a group of men standing outside the pub. We keep walking.

'Not speaking, then?'

We have to look properly now. They're young, eighteen or nineteen, and in the middle of the group is Lewis, so we go over.

'Bit of a disappointment,' Anna mutters to me.

I'm thankful to see I don't recognise any of the others, no Scott, no Norman Parks.

'Hi, Lewis!' I say.

'Hi,' he says. 'Hi, Anna. Want a drink?'

With his mates around him Lewis is looking very relaxed, nothing can threaten him, certainly not me.

'It's all right,' I say. 'We've got stuff to do.'

'So who's this, Lewis?' one lad asks.

'Bloody jailbait!' says another.

Lewis puts his arms around me, mock-defensively: 'Hands off, she's mine! Aren't you, sis?'

It's all a big pantomime for the benefit of his mates, but I let him do it – it's affection of sorts and better than the last time we spoke.

'So what're you having?' he asks again.

Simultaneously Anna says: 'Nothing, thanks!' and I say: 'A Coke!' so we stay for a Coke, standing in the sun with these beer drinkers, watching the shoppers. It feels a bit weird, as if different rules suddenly apply.

While Anna does some verbals with the lad who called us jailbait – she's got the rest of the group on her side – I try to talk to Lewis.

'Sorry about . . . you know, coming into the taxi place.'

'Forget it,' he says.

'Wish you'd come round to see us sometime. Angi'd like it.'

'What for?'

'It used to be okay; we had a laugh.'

'I have a laugh now. Never stop.' He's glancing at the others, looks as if he thinks he's missing something. I don't know, these lads laughing at my feisty mate, beer in their fists, heads back, wet mouths open – there's something a bit threatening about it. Now Lewis isn't part of the group his smile's gone.

'Might come up later,' he says, 'if there's nowt else.'

And that'll have to do; I don't want to nag him to death.

'Don't know why'm doing this,' says Lewis as we walk up Victory Street.

He was still at the pub when Anna and I finally threw in the towel and went for the bus. I don't know how much he's had to drink but he's walking okay. He's disappointed when Anna peels off into *Hair Today*; he tries to kiss her but she slips under his arm and scoots.

'Don't know why'm doing this,' he repeats as we try the door of our shop. It's locked so we go round the back.

'Hi, kid!' says Lewis to Matty who's playing on the backstreet with Diarmid. The twins seem to be practically living with Anna's mother now.

''Lo, Lewsh,' and he grins up from the complicated ramp for his brum-brum they're making from cardboard boxes.

'Angi inside?' I ask.

'Fink so,' says Matty. He's taken his tee-shirt off and his shoulders have turned red in the sun.

'Best cover up, Matty.' And he's so concentrated on what he's doing, he lets me put it on him.

No sign of Angi inside.

'Might as well go,' says Lewis. 'Don't know why'm—'

'Yes, Lewis, you already said. She'll be back soon. I'll make you a brew.'

He wanders off into the shop.

'Still a pile of junk 'n here!' he laughs. 'Anybody ever buy owt?'

'Not really,' I shout back.

'Could use a new bed, though. The one I've got stinks a bit. Stinks a lot in fact.'

'Yeah, yeah, thanks for that, Lewis!'

I can hear him moving round in the shop; he bumps into something and swears.

I take his tea in. It gives me a little shock when I see him sitting at the writing desk; he's trying to work out how to open it. I check myself, then show him how it works – can't do any harm.

'Hey, that's neat!' he says. He shuts it just so he can open it again.

He tries the little drawers, and he's so like a little kid I have to smile. I want him to be able to open the drawer that's still jammed and find something in it – an alethiometer or a plastic Indian that talks – but it stays jammed shut.

It's cool and dark in the shop, though the other side of the street is in the full glare of the sun. I can see a figure in black standing inside Mrs Pearl's shop, just looking out. What to do if you're seventy-five and live on your own?

'Ever see your dad?' I ask for something to say.

He shakes his head. 'Saw him in the pub couple of weeks back. Slipped me twenty quid. He were drunk. How 'bout you? See yours?'

'No, not for ages. I think he sends Angi money. We see Matty's dad quite a bit.'

'Liked him, Matty's dad. Pity about Matty.'

'Lewis!' I'm shocked.

'Don't start!'

'Why d'you have to say something like that?'

'Can't say nowt and you jump down my throat!'

I shut up; it was hard enough getting him here, I don't want to drive him away.

'For fuck's sake!' he says.

''M not saying owt aginst Matty!' he says.

'Love him, that kid!' he says.

'Yeah,' I say, 'though he can be a right pain; you haven't heard him on the mouth organ yet!'

And we laugh together and it's all right. We fall silent, sip our tea.

I hear a creak upstairs, someone coming downstairs, the door opening into the back room.

'Hello?' calls Angi. 'Matty?'

She giggles; it sounds like there's someone with her.

'Hi!' I call, apprehensively, wondering who the some-one might be.

'Oh, hello you!' she says, coming into the shop. Behind her is Imran.

'Hi, Lewis!' she says brightly. 'Long time no see!'

Lewis doesn't speak, just stares at her. It's pretty obvious what he thinks Angi and Imran have just been doing, and he's probably right.

Angi says: 'So what brings you up here, then? Want a brew?'

'I've made one,' I say, waving my mug, just to say something to help out.

'Remember Immy?' says Angi. ''Course you do.'

'Hi, man!' says Imran. He does a matey grin but it doesn't come easy.

Still Lewis doesn't speak.

'Ellie's let you sit at her writing desk, has she? You must be specially privileged!' Angi's starting to flag.

'Been drinking, Lewis?' she asks.

And finally Lewis speaks.

'Been shagging, Angi?'

She laughs uncertainly.

'Fucking slut!' he says, between his teeth.

She laughs again.

'Slut!'

He gets to his feet, his jaw jutting. My stomach goes tight. I think he's going to hit her.

'Okay!' says Imran. 'Okay!'

'Fucking, fucking slut!' He ignores Imran.

132

'Button it, man!' says Imran. He's getting angry; he knows it's him as much as Angi that Lewis is having a go at.

But there's no stopping Lewis; rage and beer keep him locked on the same handful of words. I can't stand it. I cover my ears and watch his clenched mouth hardly moving as he swears at Angi. I don't know how this is going to end.

Then Imran moves. He steps up to Lewis and slaps him across the face, how hard I can't tell. It's as though he's trying to bring him round rather than wanting to hurt him. Lewis staggers, surprised as much as anything, puts out a hand to steady himself on the writing desk, misses, and crashes into a glass-fronted cabinet, going down in a mess of shelves, cheap ornaments and broken glass.

He shouts in pain and puts a hand to his leg. We all watch, horrified. A china shepherdess throws herself off a tilting shelf.

'You all right, Lewis?' says Angi.

'Sorry, mate,' says Imran.

There's blood seeping out from between Lewis's fingers; it looks bad. I go over to him but he holds his other hand up to stop me.

''S okay!'

Imran says: 'Come on, I'll take you to Casualty.'

'No way!' says Lewis.

'Come on,' says Imran. 'I've got me car outside.'

''F you think I'm getting in your fucking car! Let me out of here, Ellie.'

Lewis nods towards the shop door. I open it for him.

He doesn't say another word to the other two and limps outside, getting his mobile out.

'Lewis—' I say.

'Be all right,' he says. 'I'll get someone. It's a fucker!'

He limps off down the street, dialling someone with his free hand, and doesn't look back.

Norman Parks rings up. Angi's hands are covered in some cream she's rubbing on Matty's sunburnt back so I get the phone.

'Angi?'

'No, it's Ellie.'

'*You'll do!*' which is when I realise who it is. '*What you need to know, you two fuckheads, is where I am, Boltby General A and E, that's where. Want to guess why?*'

I don't say anything.

'*I thought not. Want to guess who with? No? Well, tell Angi she's got one very poorly son in Boltby General. He's lost a lot of blood, a lot of blood. Most of it's on the seat of one of my cars – never mind that, but did you have to make him get his own cab?*'

'Imran offered—' but I stop because it sounds feeble and anyway it doesn't matter what I say.

'*Is this the guy that did it in the first place? Slices him up, then offers to help out?*'

'He didn't slice—'

'*Look; I haven't got much credit. What you need to know is they've stitched him up, given him a massive transfusion. Massive. Lewis is going to be all right, they*'

134

think. He's on a drip now, to keep him topped up with blood, drugs, dinner, the works. They think he's going to be all right. Tell Angi, if she's bothered.'

'Okay; hang on a minute—'

'When I've hung up; this is costing. But the thing is, Lewis wouldn't be with us if it wasn't for me. Want to thank your Uncle Norman, Ellie?'

He pauses.

'This is costing but I don't mind paying just to hear you say: "Thank you, Norman".'

He pauses again.

'Eh?'

What can I do? I've got to say it.

'Thanks.'

But dragging the word out is harder than being sick, harder than being sick when you've sicked up everything already.

I say: 'But you wouldn't have done it if it had been Muzz or someone...'

But, with a little chuckle, he's gone.

Angi wants to go and see Lewis. I say it's probably not a good idea after what happened this afternoon. We don't want to talk about what happened.

I say: 'What about Matty?'

Matty's all burnt and doesn't stop whingeing.

Angi says: 'I won't be long.'

I say: 'He should have had his tee-shirt on sooner.'

Angi says: 'Imran'll run me to the hospital. I won't be long.'

135

I say: 'What if Norman Parks is still there.'

She shrugs.

I say: 'And if Imran takes you...'

Angi says: 'So what?'

It's my turn to shrug. 'Don't know.'

Imran takes her to the hospital.

While she's gone I read to Matty to try and take his mind off his sunburn. He's not happy. I can feel the glow coming off his red shoulders. So I decide to try him in the cold shower.

I set it on warmish to start with, for him to get in, then turn it cooler.

'Okay, Matty?'

'More cool,' he says. 'More cool!'

And when it's the right temperature, he stands there with his eyes closed, cool water sluicing over his red shoulders and white bum and streaming off his little thingy.

'Snice!' he grins.

I leave him in the shower and sit on the landing next to the window, read a book.

He's still in there when Angi comes back. She comes up and sits next to me.

'Lewis'll be all right, they say. He's unconscious but they've got him all wired up, monitors and that. It's like "ER". He'll be all right, they're definite.'

We aren't going to talk about anything else.

'How's Matty?' she asks.

'All right. He's in there, cooling off.'

'He can't stop in the shower all night,' she says. 'What you reading?'

136

I could say it's the third in the series and what it's about is...but she's only making conversation. I've never seen Angi read a book. So I say: 'Just a book.'

'Want a drink? Coke or something?' she asks.

'Thanks.'

She hesitates.

'He wasn't there, at the hospital.'

'What?' I'm puzzled, then realise she's talking about Norman Parks: 'Oh. Him. Right.'

'I'll get that drink.'

As she's coming back up the stairs she says: 'You know what, Ellie? They've got something called Angiograms in the hospital!'

'What?'

'Angiograms; I saw a sign. What d'you think they are, then?'

'Like telegrams, only they have to be sent to Angi, to you. All of them.'

'Wouldn't that be brilliant!' And she laughs out loud, a real bellylaugh. It'd be so easy for Angi to be happy.

20

I can't sleep.

It's so hot up here and having the skylight open doesn't make much difference. I've thrown the quilt off and lie on my bed looking up at the night sky.

Angi is trying to get Matty to sleep; I can hear her voice coaxing and cajoling. However hard she tries it won't be as comforting as that cold shower; just thinking of it makes me lick my lips.

It's no good, sleep's not coming.

I do something I haven't done for ages. I walk down the bed and stand on the bedend. It's hard on your toes but it makes you high enough to stick your head out of the skylight and feel the wind on your face – except tonight there isn't any. Even the binbag stuck on the TV aerial can only manage the faintest of rustlings. The night is thick and airless. I put my hand on a slate; it's still hot.

A police siren sounds, and immediately it's answered by another, like two dogs howling, to comfort or warn each other. No reason to thinks it's anything special though.

My toes hurt and I get back in.

II: Midsummer's Day

MIDSUMMER'S DAY

This is what happened that day.

Some is what I saw, some is what other people told me, some is what I read in the newspapers – and some is me trying to get into people's heads the best I can.

You don't have to believe a word of what's written here if you don't want – go and read the newspapers if you haven't already, watch the TV, read the Inquiry report when they publish it – but I've had weeks and weeks to think about it and as far as I can tell, this is what happened that day.

So, here are the minutes of Midsummer's Day, the longest day of the year, and the longest day ever in Boltby.

*

The morning started cool. Matty had slept and though his back was still red, the fire had gone out of it, and because Matty had slept, so had Ellie and Angi.

Next door Imran slept late – after taking Angi to the hospital he still had to do six hours more taxiing. His grandfather, however, woke very early, plagued by the nightmares he had had since childhood. Muzz had a nightmare too, of the beautiful Bushra smiling at him, which only became disturbing when the camera started pulling back and Muzz realised she was standing among other people, her family, his family, in tiers like a school photograph and there were hundreds of them, and he was the photographer and he had to get away but the camera and tripod weighed a ton and the school playing field was so muddy his shoes kept getting stuck . . . and he awoke in a panic.

Next door the other way, Declan and Diarmid slept in the attic on mattresses on the floor. This wasn't meant to be a permanent arrangement but seemed to be happening to them more and more frequently. It made Diarmid uneasy; he was aware of Anna sleeping in her bedroom directly below him; recently she had begun to disturb his dreams. Right now he and Declan were rivals for the love of a Victorian mill-girl, whose disdainful features were Anna's but whose affection was reserved for a black dog that slept by the side of her loom. When he woke Diarmid immediately looked across at Declan, convinced he would be returning his worried gaze having just been shaken out of the same tormenting dream. But Declan snored gently.

Across the street Mrs Pearl slept undisturbed; her cast-iron control extended even to her sleep. All she ever dreamt of was the sea.

Across the town, in Boltby General Hospital, hooked up to monitors and intravenous drips, Lewis slept a drugged and confused sleep that became calmer with the dawn.

Taj didn't sleep. In the evening there were rumours that a gang from a neighbouring town had been spotted in Boltby and eventually Taj had caught up with them and challenged them. In the fight that followed honour was saved on both sides and no one was seriously hurt, but Taj and his three friends sat in the black car till dawn and disputed what they had done and what they should do next time. Taj thought he might get a gun that actually worked.

Another person who didn't sleep was Asif Iqbal, a taxi driver for the same taxi firm as Imran. Going off duty just before dawn he was stopped by some white men who attacked him and broke his cheekbone. He drove himself to Boltby General and rang Mrs Iqbal to say why he'd be late home.

The day started cool but by mid-morning the roof slates were already hot. Matty sat in the wardrobe in the shop, blowing his mouth organ. He had perfected a tune which went from the bottom of its range to the top, four notes, blow-suck-blow-suck.

Ellie did some hoovering to drown it out, but he was still playing the same tune when she switched off the vacuum. Eventually Anna escaped from her mother's shop and she and Ellie went downtown to make another

attempt to buy something new, which might mean
persuading themselves that yesterday's rejects were, on
reflection, just the right thing.

By mid-afternoon we're desperate for something to cool
us down and go into McDonald's for a milkshake. Eddy
Slaphead's in there with some friends. They're excited
about something. He comes over to us.

'Hi, dudes!' he says.

'How's it hanging?' says Anna. 'In fact, is it big
enough to hang?'

Eddy ignores her.

'It's kicking off!' he says. 'That's what we've heard.'

I say: 'Come again, Eddy?'

'Everybody's talking about it!'

Looking across at Eddy's friends Anna says: 'Everybody? You and your four fwends, right?' She gives a
loud slurp on her milkshake.

Eddy ignores her.

'It's starting; that's what I'm saying!'

'Eddy,' I say. 'Tell us!'

Eddy says: 'Somebody was killed yesterday, a white
guy, by an Asian. Somewhere round you, Victory Street.'

Anna says: 'Oh, yeah! So how come we haven't heard
about it?'

'It's what I've been told,' Eddy shrugs. 'Everybody's
talking.'

'Actually you've been told wrong, then,' says Anna.
'Because it wasn't just one guy, it was eleven of
them.'

'You what?' says Eddy, wide-eyed.

'It was sacrificial slaughter: Asians rounded up the Northend Under-11s Football Team and kebabed them. What I've been told.'

'Piss off, Anna!' says Eddy.

I suddenly realise what this is all about.

I say: 'Know any names, Eddy? Who this dead guy is? Who's meant to have done it?'

'"Meant to have"?' he sneers. 'Nah. All I know is this guy was surrounded by a group of Asians, told to get out of their area, then they knife him.'

'Eddy!' I say. 'If this is what I think it is, it's proper rubbish. There wasn't any gang. Nobody was killed. Nobody was stabbed, not really.'

'"Not really"? What's that mean? "Not really stabbed"? I suppose it was just a bit of surgery that went wrong.'

'Oooh! Eddy Slaphead doing sarcasm!' says Anna. 'Leave it to them who does it best, pet!'

Somebody'll stab her one day.

'Whatever.' Eddy points to his mates and says: 'Try telling them it wasn't really a stabbing.'

But they don't notice us, they're so caught up with what's happened and what they're going to do. They've gone a bit mad.

Anna and I look at each other. We can't put them straight, they wouldn't listen, and scoring points off Eddy is just a diversion.

'Eddy,' I say, 'this rumour is rubbish, believe me!'

But I do know that Lewis is at this moment lying in a

hospital bed and Eddy senses I'm holding something back.

'Whatever,' he says, 'I know what I know.'

'Good on you, Eddy!' says Anna. 'Write it down and enter it for the World's Thinnest Book Competition!'

The bus driver on the way home wants to talk.

'New gear for tonight, girls?' he says, nodding at our carrier bags. He's young for a bus driver, smiley, shaved head.

'Could only afford the bags,' says Anna. 'But there's nothing in them.'

'Tell you what,' he says. 'Dress up in them bags and nowt else and you'll drive the boys wild!'

'They're wild enough already, the boys,' says Anna. 'Don't want them no wilder.'

There are only two other people on the bus, sitting at the back: two Asian women completely covered in black.

'So, where you off tonight?' says the driver to us over his shoulder. 'GuysNDolls?'

'If we tell you, you might turn up with a mate,' says Anna. 'Try to get us drunk.'

'Might just do that!' laughs the driver.

He has to pull up fairly sharply to make the next stop; the two Asian women want to get off but haven't rung the bell. The door hisses and lets them out.

As he sets off again, our driver says: 'Must be bloody hot in them black outfits!'

I feel my stomach tighten as I wait for the next comment, which I suppose is going to be racist.

'Still, it takes all sorts,' he says.

I'm so relieved I could kiss him!

'What's this then?' says the driver, slowing as we approach The Green Dragon. There's a large crowd of drinkers spilling onto the road, their shirts off and skin burning.

In the middle is Robert Hearn, wrapped in a St George's flag, waving his glass at passing cars.

The bus driver was enjoying flirting with the two girls, or rather, with the skinny sarcastic one; the other didn't seem to have much to say for herself, a serious-looking kid.

When the two Asian women got off – he was in two minds whether to try and explain about ringing the bell – he wondered in spite of his remark whether being wrapped up in black might not be hot at all but more like being in a cool dark room. His speculation was broken by having to brake for the crowd outside The Green Dragon.

There were far too many of them to be a normal Saturday afternoon's group of drinkers. Some were familiar faces but there were some serious-looking strangers who mingled with the locals. When a silver car with a little St George's flag on its radiator drove slowly past, the crowd cheered and several of them gave stiff-armed Nazi salutes. It was a party that would turn ugly.

As the bus driver dropped the two girls at the next stop he warned them to keep clear of the pub, but instantly regretted it – it made him sound like their father. As she got off the bus the serious girl gave him such a big smile he wondered what had happened to her.

Robert Hearn saw the two Asian women get off the bus but they were too far away to bother with; in any case, here came Norman Parks doing a drive-past.

Norman flapped a hand at the people doing the Nazi salutes, wanting them to stop; it would look bad if it got in the papers. But they took no notice; everything had a momentum that was now unstoppable. You could see it shining in their faces, the call to action. Finally things were moving.

And for Norman Parks there was a little extra: he was still savouring the defeated voice of Angi's daughter thanking him for taking Lewis to the hospital. A pity she wouldn't say his name as well, that would have been...nice.

The quickest route home from the bus stop was straight past The Green Dragon but Mrs Hussein and Mrs Iqbal didn't need to consult each other to know it was safer to go the longer way round. Mr Iqbal's broken cheekbone this morning was only the most recent reminder of the need to take care.

How alcohol worked on the mind and body was a mystery to the two women. Last week Mrs Hussein had glanced through the front window to see a solitary drinker staring unhappily at a glass of amber liquid, and now grown men were bouncing around as excitably as children in a nursery, but she was as likely to taste alcohol as she was to walk round semi-naked. For some

150

reason in Britain when it warmed up to the temperature of a Pakistan winter, women older than themselves exposed their pale and lumpy flesh to the derision of strangers.

The detour taken by the two women took them past Northend Working Men's Club, where the extractor fan blew at them its mixture of stinks: beer, smoke, sweat, urine.

'Are we going to GuyNDolls, then?' says Anna as we walk back along Victory Street.

'Hey! You're not seriously interested in the bus driver, are you?'

Anna gives me a scornful look.

'Ellie! Do you mind! It's just, where else is there? Pillheads are taking over The Wearhouse, and Raffles was dead last time we went, remember?'

'I suppose.'

'Anyway,' she says, giving me a sideways look. 'He wasn't serious.'

We laugh together. It echoes up the quiet street.

'You didn't tell Eddy what happened to Lewis,' says Anna.

'No.'

Anna's the only one I've told the full story.

She says: 'You didn't even tell him it was Lewis!'

'No.'

'Well, okay if you don't want to talk about it.'

'I don't mind. I suppose I don't want the whole town talking about it.'

151

'I won't tell anybody,' says Anna.

'I didn't mean that.'

'I think she's great, your mum,' says Anna. 'Imagine: sleeping with Norman Parks *and* Imran! Nobody can say she's prejudiced!'

I just about manage to laugh.

'Don't feel bad about her, Ellie,' she says.

'It's not her I feel bad about; it's Lewis,' I say.

'He's going to be all right.'

'Yes, I didn't mean that. It's what's going on in his head. Yesterday, when Angi came into the shop with Imran, Lewis couldn't speak.'

'Well, he'd had a skinful, Ellie.'

'Yeah, but it wasn't that. I thought it was pure hate, hate squared, but now I don't know.'

'It didn't exactly sound like brotherly love.'

'No, 'course not. But it was as if he had a switch.'

'A switch?'

'Yeah, a two-way switch. One way: give Angi and Imran a hard time. And the other way: it's okay.'

'So who works it, this switch?'

'Oh, he does, and that was the problem, not with them, but with himself: which way to push the switch? But once he'd made the decision, switched it one way, he was stuck with it. Couldn't get out of it.'

Angi's outside the shop with Matty, waiting for me. Before we get to her, Anna whispers: 'Norman Parks and Imran; both St George and the Dragon! Respect!'

'Hi, Anna,' says Angi. 'I want to go and see Lewis after tea, Ellie; can you mind Matty?'

It doesn't often happen on Victory Street but there's no one around, except for Muzz's grandad standing in his doorway. The sun's got to that late afternoon angle that makes everything feel sad. If I don't go out tonight I'll die.

I say: 'We're going out, me and Anna.'

'Oh!' says Angi. 'I suppose I can take him with me.'

She'd be giving me a hard time if Anna weren't with me.

'Why not?' I say. 'Hospikles are fun, aren't they, Matty?'

Matty doesn't speak. He's been crying.

'Took his mouth organ off of him,' Angi says. 'It were driving me crazy!'

Time she did some Matty-duty.

Back on the main road there's a squeal of brakes and a big cheer goes up from the crowd outside The Green Dragon. Muzz's grandad's red beard jerks round at the sound.

It's not so far away.

Though kids stealing sweets didn't cost K Stores much financially, it made Mrs Kapoor's life a misery. If she challenged them, as often as not they cheeked her back in language that was so shameful she couldn't repeat it to Mr Kapoor when he got home from his day job.

Unlike his wife who was often reduced to tears, Mr Kapoor enjoyed working in the shop. It was more play than work for him and he happily stationed himself behind the counter, his belly filling out his white shirt, and joked with the customers. And if a kid gave him any lip, he'd swear back.

'Out my shop, little bastard!' he'd say, with a smile on his face.

K Stores was a corner shop in a poor, mainly white, area of town. Mr Kapoor thought his customers saw him as one of them, sort-of-white, rather than part of the small Pakistani and Bangladeshi community who mostly lived some distance away in the Victory Street area. He thought they were right to make the distinction; after all, the Kapoors were Indian, and were Hindu, not Muslim. He saw his faith as a relaxed, pick-and-mix religion which didn't place great demands on its followers, unlike Islam which, Mr Kapoor thought, wagged a stern forefinger. And K Stores sold alcohol and pornography; every night he had a glass or two of Bombay Sapphire gin, and turned the pages of a magazine, looking at the naked girls with what he thought was the eye of a connoisseur. Mrs Kapoor blushed for her two teenage daughters.

Because it was Saturday and Mr Kapoor only worked in the morning, he had been in the shop all afternoon. It had been a normal afternoon.

At seven o'clock in the evening a man came into the K Stores and demanded to see Mr Kapoor, who was having his dinner with his wife. He was annoyed that his daughter, Rahel, interrupted his meal, but went into the shop with a smile on his face.

'Wipe that fucking grin off your face!' said the man. With him was a kid of eight or nine, one of K Stores' regular pests.

154

'Sorry, Charlie, what is the problem?'

Mr Kapoor knew the face but unfortunately got the name wrong. The man smelt of drink. He turned to the boy and said with heavy humour: 'I'm not Charlie; are you Charlie?'

The boy shook his head and grinned.

'Neither of us is Charlie,' the man said to Mr Kapoor. 'You've got the wrong guy. But I'll tell you summat: I haven't, and if you swear at my kid again, you'll need a dentist!'

'When was this?' asked Mr Kapoor.

'You eff and blind at kids and you can't remember when – brilliant!'

'This aft,' said the boy.

'That's right,' said Mr Kapoor. 'You try to steal FHM!'

'No way!' said the boy.

'Every way!' said Mr Kapoor.

'So he's a liar; that what you're saying?' said the man.

Mr Kapoor thought of his dinner going cold; he knew he wasn't going to win here. It was a pity he couldn't remember the man's name – first-naming customers was his golden rule.

'Tell you what,' said the man. 'Let him have summat off the counter, goodwill gesture, you know?'

There was nothing new about theft, but this was outrageous: theft, open and blatant, backed up by threats from parents. If Mr Kapoor let this happen, would there be any rules left? But who could he make an appeal to?

155

The boy reached onto the counter and picked up the largest bar of chocolate.

Mr Kapoor grasped the boy's wrist and said: 'You take that, you never come in here again!'

The man said: 'You touch that kid again, you're dead!'

They left. In the doorway the boy turned and grinned, then gave Mr Kapoor the finger.

What was going on?

A little while later another kid put her head round the door and shouted: 'Free sweets!' before running off. There seemed to be a gang of children gathering outside, one or two adults too.

Mr Kapoor decided to ring the police. It was several minutes before he got an answer and the woman on the desk was very short with him.

'Sorry, Mr Kumar, but if it's only children playing around, that doesn't seem to be an emergency. I'll get someone to call round as soon as they can.'

'It isn't only children, and it's not Kumar—'

'We're extremely busy tonight, Mr Kumar, I can't tell you! Can I suggest you lock the shop and wait for assistance. Goodnight.'

Which is what Mr Kapoor did.

It's the same bus driver takes us back down into town.

'Wow!' he says when we climb on, his eyes all over us.

'At least we made an effort,' says Anna. 'Are you coming out dressed like that? Designer driver!'

'Why d'you think it's called "Diesel"?' he says.

They make a good pair, I mean, really!

He doesn't talk on the way down, though he swears at the traffic. It's slow progress. A police car screams on the road; its siren is wailing but it still can't get through. A bit comical that, like someone in a rage but unable to do anything about it. The other people on the bus keep craning their necks and looking round; we share puzzled looks.

Another police car drives up, two wheels on the road, two on the pavement.

'Keep death off the road,' says Anna. 'Drive on the pavement!'

Lewis lay in his hospital bed, fully conscious but with his eyes closed. He had been listening to the world, or at least the world of the hospital ward.

He had heard steel instruments rattle on their trolleys, the scrape of curtain rings as beds were screened off, electronic bleeping from monitors, the over-cheerful voices of visitors, the reassuring or bullying voices of the staff. In particular he had heard the confident, comforting voice of nurse Grace Pickard. He could tell it apart from all the other voices, he could tell its sure-footed approach from the far end of the ward. Even when she was talking to another patient, Lewis believed she was inquiring into his state of mind, more than that, into the state of his life. It was the most wonderful voice he had ever heard.

Nurse Grace Pickard's grandparents were from Trinidad. She was black.

This fact hadn't caused Lewis a single moment's

anguish when he first saw her; her voice had already got under his skin.

He had his eyes closed now because Grace was off-duty and not there for him to stare at, but there was a second and more immediate reason for keeping his eyes closed. Angi was sitting by his bed.

He had done the same yesterday when she had come to see him, but yesterday it had been quite easy to pretend to be unconscious; today would be harder.

Angi was alone; she hadn't brought Matty with her in the end because Diarmid and Declan called round and offered to stay with him.

'Hello, Lewis,' she said brightly to his shut-down face and sat herself on the edge of the bed. 'It's me!'

She was surprised that he was still unconscious; she understood from the desk that he had come round.

'They said you were mending; can't you hear me, Lewis? It's me, Angi.'

Lewis just lay in silence, a frown on his face.

Angi didn't know what to do. When someone was in a coma, she'd heard they played their favourite music to bring them round, 'Bohemian Rhapsody' or whatever it was, over and over again. They must do it on a walkman, Angi thought, or everyone else on the ward would go mad.

But Angi didn't know what Lewis's favourite music was. She'd sung 'Doh A Deer' to him when he was little, as she did later to Ellie and Matty, and she remembered him singing 'Wonderwall' when he was a bit older, and getting the words wrong, Ellie's dad and her laughing and making him cross.

She could just talk to him, but what about? And you've got to have someone to talk back, if you aren't going to feel stupid.

'Can't you hear me, love? It's me, Angi.'

Then, not knowing what else to do, she took his hand and looked at it, her baby's hand that was now this great big thing with bitten fingernails and ingrained dirt – presumably from his job whatever it was he did. She held his hand for a moment, then started to caress it, to stroke it, gently at first but then without thinking about it, more firmly, kneading it, working the tendons that fanned across its back, rubbing the finger joints in turn. If he'd been conscious, he'd never have let her do this.

'Sorry about everything, Lewis,' she said. 'I do the best what I can.'

Lewis opened his eyes.

'Yeah,' he said, and then, frowning: 'Angi: "doh a deer", what's it mean?'

'Search me!' laughed Angi. 'Just something to sing.'

We make our entrance into GuysNDolls.

Anna: very short like-why-bother skirt, legs up to her bum, four inches of midriff because she can, backless top – quote: *Bras? And what are they for exactly?* – nose stud, and black no-way-is-my-mother-a-hairdresser spiky hair.

Me: short*ish* skirt, merest flash of belly-button piercing and move on, plenty of uplift because *I* can, goldilocks hair that seems to work.

It's a month since we've been here, so for an instant the dark, the flashing lights and the music make it feel

159

great to be back, but once we can see into the corners, we can see there's hardly anyone in.

'Have they all moved on and not told us, Ellie?' says Anna. 'A cunning ploy to cut down the competition – and are we serious competition!'

'Maybe we've just come a bit early,' I say.

'Like these sad gets,' says Anna looking round. 'My God!'

We're surveying the place from the bar; there's no one sitting down we want to join, but standing at the bar you're vulnerable.

Here comes one now.

'Hi, girls!'

We've seen him before; actually he's not too bad.

There's some more people coming in; it's starting to fill up. Best thing to do is to leave and make a proper entrance later when there's a bigger audience.

'Tell you what,' says Anna to this guy. 'Get us those drinks later.'

He watches us go, open-mouthed; he'd never even offered.

The hundred people gathered outside The Green Dragon now made a decision, without anyone knowing how it happened or whether it needed to be argued over: it was time for the drinking and shouting and pretending to stop.

The glass that smashed on the side of a passing Asian taxi was the signal.

It was time to go!

Robert Hearn looked round for Norman Parks but he had disappeared. It didn't matter. The many-headed, many-limbed creature began to move, and it began to move towards Victory Street.

Enough!

Enough of politicians who grinned out of the TV but didn't have to live in a shithole like Boltby; enough of whoever had shut the factories; of whoever had let the streets go to rack and ruin; of whoever had let the town get like this. Whoever they were, they knew how to hide themselves away, you could never get to them.

But Victory Street, that was just a stroll away.

The police car that had been parked across from the pub speeded to the front of the group; two policemen got out and made an appeal to the group but they couldn't head it off. The policemen radioed for help and had to content themselves with kerb-crawling behind the group, headlights shining on bare calves that sometimes staggered a little but kept going.

There were spectators on the edges now, hangers-on, waiting to see what was going to happen. Robert could see Eddy Slaphead and his mates. It was a carnival, party-time, and all the better because nobody knew how it would end.

Ahead there were two police cars with their lights flashing, blocking the turning that would have let them into Victory Street, and alongside the cars more police. Dozens of mobile phones urged friends, and friends of friends, to get themselves to join the party.

Robert's mobile rang: there was something kicking off

161

at K Stores. Well, nothing was happening here yet, so go, go, go! He and a dozen others ran off down the road towards K Stores, charging down the middle of the road so cars had to brake and swerve. Tonight there were new rules: people would have to take notice of them. For long enough they'd been ignored and pushed to one side, but not tonight!

They reached a parade of poor shops – a late-night store, a take-away, a taxi firm – and it felt as though they only had to look at the windows for them to craze and shatter.

'Pakis out!' they shouted as another window went through.

Then on they ran, towards K Stores, propelled by whatever power it was that gripped them and made the streets ring.

At least that was the plan, to go back to GuyNDolls when it got more crowded, but we're sitting in BARmuda when I get a call from Muzz.

'*You all right?*' he says.

'Yeah. Why shouldn't I be?'

'*There's rumours flying about up here, gangs of racists looking for trouble. Correction: looking for Asians.*'

'Well, we're not Asian, so we'll be all right!'

'*Yeah, well, long as you're all right . . .*'

'Joke, Muzz, joke!'

'*Fuck that, Ellie. They're trying to get onto Victory Street.*'

'What d'they want to get onto Victory Street for?'

'Hey, search me, Ellie! To get to know us better, maybe, want to integrate, try me mum's curry – use your imagination!'

'Sorry, Muzz, I'm on a night out with Anna, I'm not thinking straight.'

'Thanks a bunch!' says Anna.

'Muzz, can you check if Angi and Matty are okay?'

'Well, I'm looking at the shop now and there int a light on.'

'They must still be at the hospital.'

'Got to go!' says Muzz. *'Shit me!'*

I can hear people shouting in his background, the sound of running, and tonight's theme tune: police sirens.

'Okay, Muzzy. Take care!'

But as soon as he rings off, Anna says: 'It's after nine o'clock. Hospitals throw you out well before now.'

'Trying to help me relax, Anna?'

'Just saying, Ellie, that's all. Want me to unsay it? Won erofeb...'

'Yeah, okay, okay!'

We sit for a few seconds, then I call Angi, get the anwerphone. I'm starting to panic. I ring Muzz and ask him to go round the back and check they're not in.

'I've banged on the door and shouted; they're not in!' he says: *'N-O-T I-N. Not in!'*

'Okay, Muzz, thanks.' I say to Anna: 'I'm going to have to go back, see where they are.'

'Oh, great!' she says

'You still there?' says Muzz in my ear.

'Muzz, let Anna have a listen.'

163

I hand her my phone and watch her face; she's interested.

'And that's right outside where we live, that's Victory Street!' I say.

'Okay, Ellie,' she says. 'A flying visit home, then we're back down here.'

'Muzz, is Imran around? Can he pick us up?' I say.

'*You're joking! The Asian taxi drivers are all on strike. One guy was put in hospital this morning and there's been more attacked since.*'

'Imran all right, though?'

'*Immy's got a spanner that weighs a ton under the driver's seat, so he's all right.*'

'Well, tell him to get me and Anna from BARmuda.'

'*I'll ask him.*'

'It's me and Anna, for Godssake, not some no-brains full of lager who'll jump him!'

'*I'll ask him; ring you back.*'

He doesn't.

We sit under some plastic palm leaves – each table has its palm tree growing up out of its centre – and watch what's going on. This is Saturday night, right? There should be a lot of head-flouncing and walking-about, best-smiles and quick-looks, you know, put it about a bit. But instead everyone looks like they're having real conversations about whatever it is that's broken out in the town tonight. Mobiles ring, people come in with news, go straight over to a group of mates, say what they've heard in shocked or gleeful voices; the talk's so intense it makes the clothes look ridiculous – the strappy tops and fuck-me shoes.

Muzz appears next to us.

'Come on!' he says. 'Imran dun't want to hang about.'

We stand up straight away. Everybody's looking – because of Muzz!

I want to shout: *This is Muzz! Born here, like me, if anybody's interested! Okay?* But of course I don't, just wait for Anna to say something. When she doesn't, I know it's serious.

Imran's outside with the engine running.

'Nice to have someone in the back that dun't make me nervous,' Imran says over his shoulder. 'Wouldn't have come out for nobody else. And we're going a different way, just in case.'

Imran sets off fast – but the new route's a mistake. We haven't gone far before the street's blocked off by a crowd of people gathered outside a shop: it seems to be called K Stores. I can't understand what's going on because the shop's closed. The lights are on upstairs though – they must live over – and a man's leaning out of the window, shouting down.

'What's going on?' asks Anna.

'Forget it!' says Imran, but Anna and I get out.

Imran switches the headlights off and waits in the dark with the engine running.

The shopkeeper's shouting: 'What crime is it we are committing? Open shop for you all day?'

'Hard luck, mate,' shouts someone in the crowd. 'Should get yourself a job with better hours!'

The crowd's enjoying its power, like a cat playing with a mouse.

'You want pint of milk, K Stores sells you one!' shouts the shopkeeper. 'What you want, K Stores sells you. When you want it? Breakfast time, okay; dinner time, okay; supper time, okay!'

Behind him I can see his wife, a daughter. They're terrified.

But not everybody in the crowd is hostile; some are just watching for something to do, and one or two are arguing back, defending the family.

'Y'ought to be ashamed, the lot of you!' one woman shouts. 'What've they done wrong?'

'Wrong colour!' someone shouts back.

'The Kapoors aren't Asian, they're Indian!' she replies.

'Dun't matter. They're still black!'

Kapoor? I know that name. Someone throws a cigarette packet at the man; he ducks back into the room, hitting the back of his head on the bottom of the window as he does so, but now I can see the girl behind him again. It's Rahel Kapoor from my class!

'It's Rahel!' I shout. 'That's Rahel Kapoor in there!'

'I didn't know she had a shop.' says Anna. 'Poor Rahel! But there's nothing we can do to help. Ring the police.'

Some of the crowd look round when I shout, then peer past us to where Imran's turning the car so he can get out of the street.

Someone shouts: 'Asian taxi; where did that come from? Get the bastard!'

But more stuff gets thrown at K Stores, which is enough of a distraction for us to get back to the car, but it's bad news for the Kapoors as the shop window smashes. Flames flicker inside.

Imran sets off so fast the tyres squeal.

I look out of the back window; someone throws a bottle at us and it smashes on the road. Some kids start running after us. Before we turn the corner my last image of K Stores is of Rahel at the upstairs window with her hands covering her face; I don't know if she's been hit by something, or is just crying. She won't have to do Someone Else's Shoes; her own are bad enough.

'Got to get you kids off these streets!' says Imran. 'No more stops till you're home, safe.'

Something hits the back of the car; they're still coming after us. I ring the police about the Kapoors; whoever it is I speak to says they're dealing with it and then cuts me off.

'Any other night I'd be out there!' says Imran. 'Sort them out; little bastards.'

'Big bastards, too,' says Anna.

We drive past some smashed-up shops and under the canal aqueduct – and that's as far as we get. The road's blocked, nothing's moving, and before Imran can back up, there's another car close behind us.

The car's trapped.

I wind the window down an inch, and hear shouting, the sound of running, the sound of something that's been let go, like a dog that's been let off its leash and snaps at anything in its way.

We're in its way.

Muzz's grandad watched the disturbances from his shop

doorway. He wished everyone would go home and put themselves behind strong doors, like his family, all except for his grandsons, Muzz and Imran, for whom he now waited.

How had trouble come to Victory Street?

He thought he had left violence behind a long time ago, on Amritsar railway station when he was younger than Muzz and the new Pakistan and the new India were being born. It was a bloody birth, Muslims and Hindus butchering each other for no other reason than because the other was the wrong religion. It was a madness he kept safely in the past though he couldn't keep it out of his dreams.

Victory Street had always been safe. The government ignored them and the racists had mostly stayed out. You worked hard, went to the mosque, talked to your friends in the evening, watched out for your family, and kept your head down. You expected nothing and you were content.

And now trouble had followed him here. Drunkards were baying for blood at the end of the street and the sons and grandsons of his neighbours were throwing stones at the police.

On Victory Street that was safe no longer, Muzz's grandad waited for his grandsons to come home.

And Imran shouts, 'Go!' and we're out of the car, me, Anna and Muzz, and running towards the town centre where there's bright lights and people, but all we can see is this big argument between car drivers, some are white and some are Asian, and right now they start throwing punches and there don't seem to be any police to sort it. So we stop and run back, past Imran's car – he's trying to turn it round in zero space – and run under the aqueduct, away from the centre lights and towards a row of smashed-up shops. Muzz is ahead of us because he's wearing proper trainers while Anna and I are struggling in shoes which weren't designed for the hundred metre sprint and if it's more than that we'll die. Then Muzz stops.

Ahead of us is a crowd of whites who surge towards Muzz, baying for blood.

'Get the Paki bastard!'

We turn and run back towards the centre again.

It should be funny, us running up and down the same stretch of road, but my feet are agony and I don't care any more that uplift bras aren't made for running and my heart is banging and my breath catches in the back of my throat and, no, it isn't funny at all and I know if they catch Muzz they'll kill him. Simple as that.

Muzz overtakes us as we go back under the aqueduct. I reach out and grab his arm as he goes past; I'm fading but I've had an idea.

'This way!' I gasp, and when we come out from under the bridge, I pull Muzz and Anna over to the steps which go up to the canal path.

The run up those steps finishes me off; at the top, we collapse behind the parapet. If they follow us up here, well, they do.

Muzz takes a peep over the parapet.

'Nice one, Ellie,' he says. 'We've lost them.'

I look down on the heads of the men who were chasing us. They don't think to look up; I suppose they can't hear us gasping for air, and maybe they don't know about the canal path. They mill about for a while, then get interested in Imran's car, and one starts banging on its roof.

We sit on the canal path, backs against the parapet, and get our breath back. Anna leans against Muzz and rubs her feet.

'Memo to self,' she says. 'Review Saturday night footwear.'

The canal looks inviting: glassy-black and completely still. I want to step out of the hot clammy air and into the water, walk into its depths and let the cold rise up my legs, my body and my face till there I am, gone. Away from all this.

My phone rings. It's Angi.

'*Ellie, it's me!*' she says.

'Yeah, I know it's you. Where are you?'

'*Stuck at the hospital. I've just tried Imran and I can't get him.*'

''Course you can't get him; haven't you heard about the attacks?'

'*Haven't heard anything; I've been here with Lewis. We've been talking Ellie, me and Lewis!*'

'Well, that's nice!' I say and even though I mean it, I can't help being a bit sarcastic because Angi making up with Lewis has been knocked off the top of my worry-list recently.

'*Anyway, what do you mean about "attacks", Immy hasn't been attacked, has he?*'

I can hear the banging on the car roof on the street below, and say, pretending to be more confident than I feel: 'Imran knows how to look after himself.'

Angi says: '*I suppose I'll just have to walk.*'

I say: 'It's a bit of a long way for Matty.'

'*Matty? I haven't got Matty.*'

'What?!'

'*I left him with Diarmid, er, Declan. Didn't think I'd be this long.*'

'Great! You pick your nights!'

'*Not my fault, Lewis's accident, Ellie. We've been talking.*'

'You said.'

'*Go and check Matty if you're worried about him.*'

'Angi, I'm not at home, remember. I'm on a night out.'

'*Oh, yes. Forgot.*'

'Yeah; me and Anna and Muzz are having this amazing time on the canal bank!'

'*Canal bank?*'

'Just joking.' It'd take too long to explain, and who knows – she might even be worried.

'*Oh. Anyway, I'm setting off now.*'

'So am I; see you later. 'Bye.'

''*Bye, Ellie.*'

Then I say to the others: 'Right! News update: Angi's at the hospital and apparently she's left Matty with the twins. I could strangle her.'

'Know how you feel, girl,' says Anna. 'Twins on childcare duty!'

'Come on,' I say, standing up. 'Best get back.'

'Yup,' says Anna. 'It's a bad night for Muzzes to be out.'

We run as fast as we can along the towpath, towards Victory Street.

The sun's going down, turning the sky a poisonous orange. A helicopter circles, the thudding of its rotor blades suddenly loud, then fading, as it moves. It finds something it wants and hangs for a while like a kestrel hovering; a spotlight glints like a beady eye.

Matty was sitting on the doorstep of the shop. He was alone because Declan thought he was with Diarmid, and Diarmid thought he was with Declan.

Matty didn't mind not being with anyone because things kept happening. There was shouting and flashing lights and running.

The old woman in black came out of her shop and asked him where his sister was and where his mother was and did he want to go into her house. He said no, but she didn't seem to like that answer. She said she would go and find someone and she went.

Another time some big boys ran down the street, laughing and shouting. One shouted: 'Yo, Matty!' at him and he shouted, 'Yo!' back but the boy didn't stop. Another time soon after two police vans went the same way as the boys and they ran back, not laughing.

'Yo!' Matty shouted but no one replied. He got up and followed them but they went too fast and were gone.

172

At the far end of the street were bright lights and people shouting. There were some policemen with big boots on and helmets with windows in front of their eyes. Why were they hiding? One of them said to Matty: 'Fuck off out of it, kid!' So he went and sat on the kerb in a side street, pushing his brum-brum up and down the pavement. He didn't see Ellie or Angi or the old woman in black.

Another time he wanted a wee so he went round the corner and did it and in the middle of doing the wee he heard some people coming down the street he was on. They were coming out of the dark and one of them was Huggy!

He ran back onto the big street, blowing his mouth organ, and some people ran up the side street and started hitting. Everybody was running about and shouting. A policeman said: 'You shouldn't be out, kid!' but Matty didn't know if it was the same one as the other time.

There were some cars on the street and suddenly one of them wasn't there but a big wump! of fire and then the car was there again but all black and smoky. A fire engine came through and they squirted on the car.

The night was smelly.

What have they done to my street? It's wild and glaring and angry.

Victory Street has become a huge hall filled with strange lights, confused shouting, and a smell like bonfire night mixed with a splash of petrol. Another helicopter has joined the first and their thudding rotors overhead sound like a roof being nailed into place. The road runs with oily water, reflecting the flames of burning cars and pulsing police lights, and there seem to be banks of extra floodlights too. A voice shouts at us over a loudhailer, urging us to do something, or stop doing something, but we can't tell what – it just echoes off the walls and adds to the clamour.

Nobody's listening. Some people huddle in little groups, watching in disbelief; others argue, with each other or the police. There's a large group who are taunting the police and sometimes the police go after someone in a flurry of action that makes the crowd cheer and clears a space for a minute. It looks like a weird kind of dance, but it isn't – it's just total confusion.

'At last! A bit of action for the camera!' says Anna, pointing up at the CCTV camera. It swivels round, taking note. Some lads chuck stones at it but their aim isn't good enough. They run off as a police car screeches towards them; four policeman jump out.

'You!' shouts one of the policemen, pointing at us. 'Get off the street!'

'We live here!' Anna shouts back.

'Get bloody inside, then!' he yells, but he's more interested in catching the stone-throwers. They chase them across the children's play area, dodging through the swings and roundabouts. They've nearly got away when one of the lads fails to see the metal pole supporting the swings and runs smack into it. He goes down as if he's been shot and the police are on him like

174

dogs catching the fox. They drag him, unconscious, back to the car. A wooden horse's head rocks to and fro behind them.

'Hey, guys!' says a voice behind us.

It's Eddy Slaphead, on his own, glad to see us.

'Eddy!' says Anna, gesturing at the scene in front of us. 'You said it was kicking off today; this what you had in mind?'

Eddy stares and doesn't reply. He looks shocked, scared even.

The policemen are right in front of us now, their breath rasping from the chase, frogmarching this lad they've caught. His face is grey and there's a dark weal on his forehead. I know him. He's not a bad lad.

Eddy stares, his mouth open.

The policeman turns on us. 'I said: "Move it!"' and pushes Eddy so hard he staggers and nearly falls.

'Sorry!' Eddy says, as though it's his fault, but the policeman's got into the car with the others.

'All part of the fun,' says Anna. 'When things kick off, Eddy, you don't know who's going to get kicked.'

Muzz cuts in: 'Anyway, man, who you with?'

'Me?' says Eddy. 'On me own. I lost the others.'

'No, I didn't mean that!' says Muzz, an edge to his voice. 'I meant, are you with them?'

'Them?' says Eddy.

'Yeah. Are you with them down the end of the street? The racists. Them. Or are you with us?'

Eddy doesn't say anything, just looks at me a bit hurt that I passed on what he said in PSS.

'He's not with anyone,' says Anna. 'You're just here for the laugh, aren't you, Eddy?'

Behind us a window smashes, the bits rattling onto the pavement, and a cheer goes up. We spin round.

It's Mrs Pearl's shop window.

'Oh, no! Not Mrs Pearl's!'

There's group of a dozen or so teenagers just beyond Mrs Pearl's; they're the ones who cheered, though I can't tell if it was them who put it through.

'Why'd they do that? Mrs Pearl never hurt anyone.'

Anna says: 'You want reasons, Ellie? Tonight? With all this going on, you expect logic?'

In the middle of the group I can see Taj and some of his mates. They spot us and start running towards us.

'Berra go,' says Eddy and starts to move.

But Muzz grabs his arm.

'It's okay, man,' says Muzz. 'Relax.'

Eddy says: 'I gorra go!' and he tries to break free but Muzz won't let him.

'It's cool!' he says, and he is cool, though I can see from the strain in his fingers what an effort it is to restrain Eddy. It's the most physical I've ever seen Muzz, and I don't like what he's doing, because when Taj gets hold of Eddy, well, I hate to think what he'll do. Eddy is bricking it.

But now we'll find out.

'Nice one, Muzz!' says Taj, running up, and as usual ignoring me and Anna. 'Where d'you catch this guy? Do we know him?'

176

They're all round us now. Muzz relaxes his grip on Eddy; he isn't going anywhere.

'You boys are up late tonight!' says Anna to defuse it, but Taj just ignores her.

Taj says to Eddy: 'Where you from? Not round here.'

Eddy manages to whisper: 'No, 'm not.'

'Just visiting, then? Holiday kind of thing?'

Taj's mates all snigger at this, and Eddy does his best to be look amused, but he's terrified. Even with the red glow from the burning cars, his face is white as paper.

Taj says: 'You can stop smiling. Tin't no holiday. You're with them bastards, innit!'

There's nothing I can do.

'Taj, meet Eddy,' says Muzz, offering him up.

Taj holds out his hand, and says: 'Pleased to meet you, Eddy.'

I know if Eddy responds, if their paws touch, that'll be it: he'll get his head kicked in.

Taj stands there with his hand held towards Eddy, a faint smile on his mean, handsome face.

Then Muzz switches it. He says: 'Yeah, he's a mate from school, Eddy is.'

'Oh?' Taj says, without moving.

'Yeah. A good mate. Came up to see me tonight.'

'Don't believe you, man!' says Taj.

'Suit yourself. Whatever. Picked a good night, didn't you, Eddy?' says Muzz, and he even manages this stupid, goony laugh, and Eddy joins in.

'Hey, Taj!' says one of his mates. 'Let's kick the shit out of him anyway. White bastard!'

Muzz says: 'There's three of them, three white bastards. There's Anna and Ellie, too – so what you saying?'

It's going Muzz's way now, and his timing is brilliant. He lets his last comment hang in the air for a couple of seconds, long enough for it to be obvious that Taj doesn't know what to do next, and then Muzz puts his hand on Eddy's shoulder – the same hand that stopped Eddy doing a runner a minute ago – and begins steering him away.

'Come and meet me grandad,' he says to Eddy. He wills the circle of Taj's mates to open to let them through – and they do.

Anna and I follow.

'God, Muzz!' I say when we're out of earshot. 'You like living dangerously!'

Anna says: 'I think you'll find it was me and you and Eddy who were living dangerously, not Muzz!'

But we're talking to the back of their necks and neither of them says a word till Taj and his sidekicks decide to move on, racing back to the pushing and shoving at the frontline.

Then Muzz stops, turns Eddy to face him.

'Explain it again, Eddy,' he says. 'About them and us. I'm still not clear which is which.'

'I got to go,' says Eddy. 'Please.'

He looks like he's going to be sick.

'Please.'

Then he *is* sick; he bends over and retches. And hardly so's you can see it, Muzz pats his back, same hand.

'Okay,' he says. 'Okay, Eddy. Meet me grandad another night.'

And Eddy stands up, pulling a long strand of sick from his mouth with his fingers, and nods slowly.

'Moff home,' he says, and walks off, face pointed down. He's seen more than enough tonight and nothing's going to keep him here any longer. Even when a man with blood pouring down his face staggers towards Eddy, it doesn't deflect him, he just keeps going, even when he's confronted by a patch of road that's burning. How can that be? Roads are cold and hard, but it's got flames dancing on it like a Christmas pudding, I swear.

Nothing's going to surprise me tonight.

'Best see if Mrs Pearl's all right,' I say.

'And I'll check the twins aren't murdering Matty,' says Anna, waving at a figure at the window of her flat. So far the windows of *Hair Today*, *Angi's Antiques* and *Aslam's General Store and Grocery* are unbroken but I don't know how long that'll last.

There aren't any lights on in Mrs Pearl's. I peer in through the hole in the window, glass crunching and squeaking underfoot, and call her name, but nothing happens.

When I go round the back it's a complete blackout and banging on the door doesn't achieve anything; Mrs Pearl's not here.

Anna's on the front street already – with her mum.

'They haven't got Matty!' says Anna.

'What!'

'Ellie, I didn't even know the twins were meant to be looking after Matty,' says Anna's mum who's really upset. 'I could strangle them.'

'Strangle Angi, more like!' I say.

'Don't say that,' she says. 'She's got a lot on... with Lewis and everything.'

But I think she half agrees with me.

'So! Matty's out here somewhere. Great!' I say.

And I'm about to suggest we spread out to find him when there's a great roar from the crowd and all the kids who've been yelling at the police come flying towards us down the road.

The police are charging them, banging their shields with their batons.

We scatter before we get flattened.

Scott had his mobile phone to his ear. Norman was saying something but Scott had stopped listening; the action on Victory Street was a thousand per cent more interesting.

The firemen had given up trying to put out the fires and were trying to defend themselves from the stones raining down on them, and the police had stopped trying to keep the whites out and were now concentrating on keeping the Asians in, who were running around like frightened chickens.

One kid came towards him, blowing a mouth organ of all things! He saw the kid wasn't Asian but white, and was Down's syndrome. Scott vaguely thought he knew him – but then, one Down's kid was pretty much like another, Scott thought. The boy turned and ran off, blowing his mouth organ even more urgently.

'TV cameras there yet?' asked Norman in his ear. 'I've just spoken to them, told them what's going on. Deplored the fact my taxis aren't running tonight for fear of attack from Asian thugs.'

He chuckled.

'It's totally mad here!' said Scott. 'You should get yourself round – nobody'll notice.'

Norman was parked up a few blocks away. He'd decided that it wouldn't be a good idea if he were spotted in the middle of the riot so he'd told Scott to be his eyes, keep him updated. Scott thought that for a leader Norman was surprisingly timid; he was pretty good at setting everything up – and then doing a disappearing act.

'I'll think about it,' said Norman.

Lewis was missing too, of course, and Scott wondered if it was more than the 'stabbing' that had kept him away. Recently he'd been making excuses for not joining in on leafletings for the Knights. Norman would have to talk him up.

People came and went: that guy with the blood pouring down his face; ten minutes ago Scott had seen him laughing his head off. And that lad wiping his mouth with the back of his hand – didn't he know him from somewhere? It was like a mad party, familiar faces swimming into view, then disappearing: laughing, and when you next see them, crying; dancing like crazy one minute, and next minute with their head down the toilet.

A stone skittered past Scott's feet, another ricocheted off the wall above him. He jumped back into a doorway as the police charged down the street, banging their shields.

As he watched he saw there was a little group of whites in the path of the police and the retreating Asians. They dived out of the way, one, a blonde girl, coming to Scott's side of the street.

No doubt about that face: it was Lewis's kid sister, tarted up for a night out, but looking a right mess now. She ran along the pavement towards him, then disappeared down a side street out of the way of the surging crowd.

Scott rang Norman back, then came out of his doorway and sauntered towards the street she'd gone down.

No surprise to see Scott here tonight: Norman Parks' gang helping things along. He didn't see me, but I can't even be bothered to think about him – it's Matty I'm after.

'Matty? You there?'

It's much darker here and walking away from the main street with all the yelling behind me, it's quiet enough for him to hear me, if he's down here.

'Matty!'

No reply, and no sign of anyone else either. I suppose everyone's either up on Victory Street, watching the action, or else they'll have locked themselves inside.

'Matty!'

The thing about Matty is he doesn't always answer

even when he knows you're looking for him. He can be sitting on a step ten feet away, looking up at you, grinning, and not saying a word.

'Can you hear me, Matty?'

I can't see to the end, but there's no point in going all the way down here; he won't have gone too far from Victory Street. I stop and give it one more double-strength: 'Matty!'

Silence; no movement in the shadows. I turn to go back – and there's someone in the end of the street, silhouetted by the blaze of Victory Street. He's sauntering towards me, taking his time, but definitely coming after me.

I know who it is.

I turn away and walk down to the first backstreet, and as soon as I reach it, I run like hell into its gloom. Scott's going to be faster than me, if he decides to come after me, but I'm sure I know these streets much better than him.

Halfway along I know exactly where to do a right-angle turn into a little alleyway – and go over on my heels!

I sit on the ground, scrabbling around for my left shoe which has come off. When I find it and try to put it back on, the strap's broken. There's nothing for it; I take the other one off, stand up and carry on barefoot. But on the plus side, he can't hear me now, and I can hear him: the soft, urgent tread of running footsteps which is no longer the sound of someone sauntering. Then he suddenly stops, unsure of which way to go, and when the footsteps start again they're less urgent. He's missed this turn.

I walk to the far end of the alley, carrying my shoes and hoping I don't cut myself or stand in something.

It's irritation I feel more than anything else: there's a riot going, Matty's missing, but here I am dodging about the back alleyways, in the dark, barefoot, trying to shake off a twat like Scott. Well, at least I've managed to do that: his footsteps have faded completely into the background din of Victory Street.

I turn towards the side street where I first started looking for Matty. Basically I've just run three sides of a big square, and the soles of my feet are starting to hurt. A stone only needs to be the size of a rice krispie to give you pain when you put your bare heel on it, so I've discovered. I stop and lean on a backyard wall, and put my shoes back on – which is a relief, never mind the broken strap. Before I walk on, I'm puzzled by a tiny red light in the window of the house whose wall I've been leaning on. It glows brightly, then fades. I realise it's someone smoking a cigarette.

It glows again, and it's with a shock I see there's a whole family at the window, dark figures staring out: father doing the smoking, wife by his side and five or six kids below them, the littlest with their chins on the windowsill, dark figures watching me. As far as they're concerned, I could be anybody. Tonight I could be someone about to throw a brick through their window. To show I'm not, I wave, which when you think about it is pretty pointless. Hi! I'm your friendly right-on neighbour, just keeping an eye on things!

Not surprisingly, they don't wave back. The cigarette

glows again as he takes another draw. One family, like hundreds of others, that daren't come outside and daren't go to bed either.

Nothing I can do and I can't keep prying into someone's back room.

I start to walk on, and out of the corner of my eye I see a movement in the shadow.

'Matty?'

Quick running footsteps, then a hand grabs my arm roughly. Not Matty.

A man's voice: 'Hey! It's Lewis's kid sister!'

Scott.

'Get off me!'

He's not letting go, however hard I tug.

'Cool it!' he says.

I wop him in the face with my spare hand, a sort of slap-punch that makes him angry.

'I said: Cool it, you little bitch!'

He grabs my free hand and pushes me against the wall. I turn my face away from the stink of Lynx and cigarettes.

'You look lost,' he says. 'Damsel in distress.'

I know the theory: knee him where it hurts, but he's right against me and I can't move.

'Well, you're in luck. St George to the rescue.'

'I don't need anything from you!' I say between my teeth.

He's really hurting.

'Oh, I think you do!' and he tries to make it sound sexy.

I don't know what to do. I don't know where this is going. I feel a twinge of fear in my stomach.

'Best thing is stop fighting,' he says close to my ear and I cringe because I think he's going to kiss me. If he does, I'll be sick.

I keep my face averted, looking towards the side street. It's not that far away. Light shines down it from Victory Street. If I can make it to there...

As I watch, a silver car glides out of the dark, silently as a shark, and stops. Even from here I can see it has a little St George's flag on the front.

A man in a black leather coat climbs out.

'You're really in luck,' says Scott. '*Two* St Georges!'

Norman Parks walks round to this side of the car, opens the passenger door, and stands with one hand on the door, looking towards us.

This is no accident; it's been organised over their mobiles. So whatever's going to happen next will be organised too.

I shout.

Immediately Scott claps a hand over my mouth, spins me round and forces my arm up my back.

'Shut it!' he growls. 'Come and meet Norman.'

He pushes me down the street towards the open door of the silver car. Norman Parks just watches with a look of disdain on his face.

I can't out-wrestle Scott.

When we get to the car Norman Parks says to Scott: 'Let her go.'

'You what?'

'I said: Let her go.'

Scott does, but there's no point in me trying to make a run for it.

'Get in,' Norman Parks says, jerking his head towards the car. The engine's still running.

'No way!'

'Don't worry, I'm not going to do anything to you,' he sneers. 'Unlike some people, I've got a reputation to keep.'

He pushes me into the car, slams the door, goes round to the driver's side and gets in. But instead of driving somewhere, he switches the engine off.

Scott loiters outside, standing guard.

'I just want to have a little talk, okay?'

'There's nothing to talk about,' I say.

'Isn't there? Beg to differ, sweetheart. Look at that!'

He points straight ahead at the slice of Victory Street at the end. It's like being in a dark cinema and the screen is Victory Street, a blaze of light and action, figures running about. As I watch, Anna runs across, her mother behind her, but even if I opened the door and yelled, it would be too far, they wouldn't be able to hear me.

'Bit of a mess, that!' he says. 'If you ever wanted a demonstration of how the races can't mix, there it is. Racial harmony – what a joke!'

'And whose fault's that?'

'Nothing to do with me, sweetheart. I'm just sitting here minding my own business.'

He turns to me, but I don't want to look at him.

'Leave us alone and we'd get on fine!' I say, thinking

of the dark figures in the back window, the little red glow. 'We don't need you lot stirring it. That slimeball, Scott, and his mates.'

'You mean like Lewis, mates like that?'

I don't reply.

He says: 'That seat you're sitting on, feels damp does it? I had to get it valetted yesterday, get the blood out of it. Know why that was?'

I don't reply.

'All right, if you don't want to speak, you'll just have to listen. None of this would have happened if your slapper of a mother was a bit more particular about who she shags!'

'I don't have to listen to this!' I say, reaching for the door handle.

'Oh yes, you do!'

He grabs my arm, and I look at him now.

'Whites and Asians, they don't go together. No argument about it. They shouldn't mix, because it's not going to work, understand? They shouldn't live together, they shouldn't go to school together, they shouldn't work together, because it's nothing but trouble. And what they really should not do is go to bed together. That's just disgusting!'

He speaks quietly, almost in a whisper, so the words come hissing out. I can't work out what it is about whites and Asians getting on with each other that frightens him, but he's so fervent about it. It's deranged him.

He goes on: 'The sooner they build a wall round

this part of town, the better. They should get everybody on the right side of it, with their own kind.'

I say: 'So I can't live next door to Muzz? That's a problem, is it?'

He's hardly heard me. 'Whites and Asians; you know, they don't even go in the same sentence!'

What can you say to that kind of madness?

'So,' he says, 'anybody who crosses the line – Angi and whatever his name is – anybody who does that, had better watch their backs. They'll get sorted.'

We sit in silence, staring ahead. It's bizarre: Norman Parks, the man I hate most in the world, and me sitting side by side in a car, like an old couple parked up in a lay-by having a Sunday afternoon snack.

Scott grins into the car and makes a filthy gesture.

Norman Parks turns to me again.

'So just tell Angi, all right? And anybody else who feels tempted: don't cross that line. We'll sort them out. Okay?'

'I'm not your messenger. Angi can do what she likes.'

He laughs: 'Yes; I know she does. The whole town knows it.'

Then I have a thought, a shot in the dark.

'She didn't finish with you, Angi, did she? For Imran?'

Though he reckons to laugh again, I know I've hit on the truth, and it's my turn to laugh.

'She did, didn't she!'

He doesn't speak.

Yeeessss!

And while I'm feeling good, without planning it, I say: 'You're not going to win, you know.'

'Oh no?' he says. 'So who's going to stop us?'

And without thinking how ridiculous it sounds, I say: 'Me and Muzz.'

But he doesn't laugh, just says: 'You know; you're sick, like Angi. Sick. Come on! Get out of my motor.'

This is so sudden I don't move.

'That's the handle, there. Out!'

Well, that's fine by me, so out I climb. As soon as I'm on the pavement Scott comes towards me, leering, and planning I don't know what, but Norman Parks just shouts from inside the car: 'Scott! Leave her alone. You stupid or something?'

Scott stands there with his mouth open.

Norman Parks calls: 'See you, sweetheart! Get back to your black bastard friends!'

I don't need telling again.

In two minutes I'm back on Victory Street, and remembering what I'm meant to be doing: finding Matty.

I go towards the police lines, nearly bumping into a well-dressed stranger talking to himself – but then I see it's a reporter who's speaking into a microphone and making eyes at a TV camera perched on a cameraman's shoulder. He's talking TV reporter-speak: '...flames of racism...tonight a sleepy northern town has exploded ...completely out of the blue...excitable Asian youths ...baffled residents...'

That's enough; I know Norman Parks won't get a mention. Come to Boltby for more than ten minutes, mister reporter man, and you'd understand better.

A shout goes up at the police line; a fight's broken

out, a kid punching and kicking a policeman in full riot gear.

The kid's Matty.

Police constable Miles Bentley was not in the best of moods. He had been planning to have a few friends over for a barbecue tonight but suddenly all leave had been cancelled and here he was instead: in a miserable part of a miserable town in the middle of a riot.

For the first hour they had been keeping drunken racists out, which had worked, except some of them had gone off and smashed up shops in other parts of town. Things seemed to be calmer for a while until some racists took refuge in a pub, and the next thing, whoom!, it had been firebombed. Firemen were battling with it now.

Now the Asians clamoured to get out so they could sort out the racists. No, thought Miles, you don't want to do that. It might seem like a good idea on Saturday night, but in court on Monday morning it will look bad, bad, bad. So now the police were having to contain the jumpy Asian crowd, and getting no thanks for it. Miles Bentley had been hit by several stones.

And in the middle of it, there was a bloody kid blowing a mouth organ! The same non-tune, over and over.

'Here; cut it out, you little...' said Miles.

The kid ignored him, or didn't hear. He came closer, still blowing.

Miles Bentley had had enough. He reached out, grabbed the mouth organ, and stuck it in his pocket.

'I warned you, son!' he said. 'That's it, now! Finito!'

He didn't expect what happened next. The kid, who was only young but built like a brickshithouse, came flying at him, kicking and hitting. It didn't really hurt, of course, but in the middle of a riot, a policeman being attacked could be the spark for open war. And it wasn't just a policeman, it was him! Miles grabbed the boy by his shoulders.

'Stop it right there, son. Or else!'

This had got silly; he was busy enough without threatening kids with arrest. Miles Bentley closed his eyes and counted to three. When he opened them again he was staring at a girl with dirt or mascara smeared across her cheek.

'What you doing?' she demanded of Miles. 'It's only Matty.'

'Silly me!' said Miles. 'I should have known!'

'Let him go,' she said. 'Please.'

Miles thought she was close to tears.

'Okay, love. Take him home, and explain to him that kicking and punching isn't a good idea. Especially when it's me.'

She took the boy by the hand and led him away.

Now PC Miles Bentley could turn his attention back to the state of play down the street. The crowd wasn't getting any smaller. Miles wished the firemen would turn a waterhose on them, cool them down, send everybody home, and if that meant they had to let the pub burn to the ground, well, he was past caring. One miserable pub less in this miserable town.

Across town the bus driver wasn't going to make it to his favourite pub. The hold-up had made him too late; he would have to stay in. He showered, got a beer from the fridge and channel hopped. He saw a reporter standing in what looked like a war zone somewhere and had already pressed the button for another channel when he thought he heard the reporter say: 'Boltby.'

And now he saw it wasn't a war zone but a street he knew, but looking all wrong, a garish red, like a familiar face smeared with blood.

The bus driver stared at the scene, mesmerised. How had this started? He remembered the volatile and threatening crowd outside The Green Dragon but there didn't seem to be any pictures of that – maybe it was too early, before the TV cameras arrived.

Then on the screen appeared a face that was familiar – how did he know her? She was walking past the camera when the reporter threw a question at her and she faltered and looked at the camera which zoomed in on her face so it filled the whole screen. There were tears in her eyes, but she looked angry as much as sad.

'Leave us alone!' she said. 'It was okay before; we don't need this. Come on, Matty. Let's go home.'

And she turned away and walked down the wet, shining road towards the fires, hand in hand with a boy.

The reporter said: 'And that's what a lot of residents are thinking tonight in Boltby, that these Asian rioters are tearing apart a community that till tonight was at peace with itself. This is Mark Irving, handing you back to the studio.'

Where had he seen the girl before? The bus driver couldn't remember. He shook his head and went to the fridge for another beer.

The TV cameras missed the reappearance of Scott who had ignored Norman Parks' instruction that he get off the street and go home.

He was walking along the pavement towards the police lines when he caught sight of Ellie and consequently failed to notice a small but hazardous object lying in wait for him: Matty's brum-brum, forgotten in the excitement of the night. It roller-skated Scott's foot along the pavement and down he went, cracking his elbow on the stone flags.

He broke the bone called the humerus, but he didn't laugh.

It's ending.

The police are back in control and everybody knows it; they're starting to drift back inside, like us.

We're watching from Anna's upstairs, all of us. Angi finally made it back from the hospital after being stuck on the wrong side of the police lines, and Diarmid and Declan have been told off, big time, by everybody, but they haven't gone off in a sulk; they want to be here. We all want to be together, for a while, as things quieten down. We can still hear the drumming of the helicopters overhead, but the street is clearing. The firemen are finishing off, watched by the few people who are still out on the street. Down below we can see Muzz's grandad with some of his friends. Their faces give nothing away. Two of them hold hands and speak earnestly together. After all the fighting and shouting, I love them, these quiet old men.

Mrs Pearl is up here with us too, and because it's such a strange night, that doesn't seem odd.

There must be twenty other windows that have been put through tonight besides hers, including Muzz's, but not ours or Anna's mum's. There are rumours about who's done it and why. The answer seems to be: nobody in particular, for no particular reason, just the general craziness of the night. I know for a fact, because I saw him, that Javed put his *own* window through, so how crazy is that?

In a way it should be worse for Muzz's family than for Mrs Pearl because theirs is a working shop and it'll take forever to pick the broken glass out of the tomatoes and onions and potatoes, whereas Mrs Pearl's shop is empty.

Matty's falling asleep against Angi. She comes off the mobile.

'Still can't get hold of Immy,' she says. 'Just wanted to say night-night.'

It's the third time she's tried him tonight that I know of – Angi, you'll only put him off!

'I suppose we should be thinking about bed,' says Anna's mum. 'Look at the time!'

She's right. Matty's nearly asleep on his feet and the twins are flagging too.

'I suppose,' she hesitates, 'you could all bed down here, if you felt, you know, you wanted to.'

Anna looks at her mum as if she's gone mad, but Angi's up for it.

'Yeah, it'd be nice to be . . . together,' she says.

Somebody's got to take control.

'Thanks,' I say, 'but Matty needs his own bed, his own bits, so we'd best go home.'

'Suppose so,' says Angi, disappointed.

'My grandad says I've to help get the shop sorted, make it safe before tomorrow,' says Muzz. Well, nobody said the offer of sleep-over didn't include him, so good on you, Muzz.

'You're opening tomorrow?' asks Anna incredulously.

'I dunno,' says Muzz. 'Why not? We open every day, always do.'

Mrs Pearl says: 'And the old lady will go back to her own house, thank you very much. But she would thank Eleanor to accompany her across the road.'

Anna lets us out through the shop. The two hair dryers sit there in the dark. And honestly, the way things are, I wouldn't have been surprised if they'd spoken, but they keep their heads down.

Angi and Matty go through the shop door – Matty's so tired he's staggering – and Muzz walks over to where his grandad is waiting patiently. He puts a hand on Muzz's shoulder and smiles at me.

The smell of burning still wafts about and I can hear the quiet clunkings of people tidying up and making running repairs before they go to bed.

Mrs Pearl isn't going to make any repairs tonight. We stand in front of her shop and gaze at the gaping hole in the window; the glass lies shattered on the pavement and inside the shop.

'Sure you'll be all right? You could stay with us,' I say, knowing she'll say no.

'Ellie, once before I let myself be forced out of my home, and I couldn't go back. Never again. When you get to my age you have nothing to fear, so tonight I sleep in my own bed. Thank you.'

'Okay, Mrs Pearl.'

What's she doing now? She's bending over, taking off one of her shoes, as if she's got a stone in it.

'Don't cut your foot on the glass,' I say, and feel stupid, as if I have any idea what's she's doing anyway.

Then she puts it back on and stands upright. I can dimly see she is holding the little twist of paper from her shoe.

'I showed you these before, my father's last gift to me, my insurance. He was a man who believed in insurance.'

She laughs and opens up the twist of paper. I see the tiny gems gather up to themselves the bit of light left on Victory Street, glittering in the folds of the paper. For the first time I can understand why there's a fuss about diamonds.

'Let them pay for the breakage!' she says.

And she flings them into the broken glass of her shop window.

When does a day end? At midnight? When people go to bed?

Midsummer's Day ended eventually, and cool again, with most people in the beds they had started the day in.

Mrs Pearl slept soundly in spite of a shattered shop window.

Matty was so tired he fell asleep before he had time to register the loss of his two most precious possessions: his mouth organ, which was still in PC Miles Bentley's pocket, and his brum-brum, which was lying in the gutter, its wheels bent from being stood on. It would be swept up in the next few days' cleaning operation.

It was well after midnight when Scott got to bed. The hospital was busy and it was several hours before his elbow could be X-rayed and set.

Not far from Scott in the hospital, Lewis slept in the bed he hadn't left for two days. Even if he were allowed visitors at two in the morning and even if Scott had felt like going to see Lewis, he would have been wasting his time. Lewis will speak only briefly to Scott and to Norman Parks again: two days in a hospital bed had given him time to think.

In his flat over St George's Taxis, Norman Parks watched 24-hour TV news till well after midnight, with great satisfaction. Stupid Asian kids caught beautifully on camera, throwing stones, fighting the police, rioting. Talk about being left holding the baby, the dirty nappy! Not that Norman Parks knew anything about dirty nappies. You'd never trace the stink of anything unpleasant to him.

He began to plan what he would say in the TV interview he'd already lined up for the morning: lay the blame firmly at the door of the Muslims . . . proved once again that multiculturalism didn't work . . . time for white people to stand up to the politically correct town council...time to end favourable treatment for ethnic minorities.

Norman Parks sipped his tea and marvelled at how you could get away with talking complete rubbish.

The Kapoors slept, very fitfully, not in their beds but on the floor and settees of a friendly couple who lived two streets away from the burnt-out K Stores. All night, her arms wrapped around her younger sister, Rahel whispered words she hoped comforted her sister even if she couldn't believe in them herself.

Robert Hearn and Taj slept soundly, unaware their faces, blurry but recognisable, had been stored by the CCTV cameras and would soon be printed up with others in the local newspaper under the headline DO YOU RECOGNISE THESE HOOLIGANS?

One person did not sleep that night: Muzz's grandad. He had sent Muzz to bed, telling him the clearing up could wait till the morning and he would keep watch. He sat, a dark shape in the dark shop, completely immobile, and waited for Imran to come home.

For Muzz's grandad, Midsummer's Day did not end with midnight, or with bed and sleep. It will never end. He didn't yet know that Imran was sitting in his car in a disused factory yard on the edge of town, staring at the eastern sky which was getting brighter with the dawn.

He was staring without seeing.

The top of his skull had been smashed by the iron bar which the police will find thrown over the factory wall. Under his blood-soaked seat Imran's heavy spanner lay untouched; the three men who forced him to make that dismal last drive ensured he didn't have a chance to defend himself with it.

The mobile in Imran's pocket bleeped faintly as Angi, waking suddenly, sat up in bed, texted him, then lay down again.

III: A New Story

1

We're in the storeroom at the back of Muzz's shop – there's a tray of melons going rotten and waiting to be chucked out – and he's just told me about the school-photograph Bushra dream he keeps having.

'It's only because she's an unknown quantity,' I say.

'Known quantity is she's got three big brothers, Pakistani mafia, who'll slit my throat if I step out of line.'

'Thinking of stepping out of line already, Muzz? You're not even married yet!'

'Got to plan ahead, man!' he says with a grin.

His grandad comes in and we shut up.

Over a week has gone by and he still can't get Imran's body for burial. Muzz says Muslims have to have the funeral as soon as possible, the day after if they can, but

203

the postmortem hasn't been done yet. He said in a hot country they'd have had the burial by now. I said right now this is a hot country. He said they're keeping the body in a big fridge. I imagine Imran lying there with a dusting of frost on his face. I'm glad he's nice and cool, if he can't be alive.

Muzz's grandad says something in Punjabi and looks at me.

Muzz says: 'He'd like to say something to you.'

He speaks in a quiet, measured way, stopping every now and again so that Muzz can translate into English for me. I can tell Muzz isn't that brilliant at Punjabi because he has to rerun some words with his grandad. Like I'm brilliant at Punjabi, of course!

'He says he has lived a long time and there has been much grief in his life.'

I nod.

'He says you know he has lost Imran but he would like to tell you that there have been other losses in his life.'

It's cheering up I need, but there's nothing I can do.

'He says he wasn't much older than me when his father died, was killed at the time of Independence – he means when Pakistan and India became independent from Britain,' says Muzz off his own bat.

His grandad pauses – he looks a bit surprised by how much Muzz has to say – but then starts again.

'He says his own son – that's my dad – died because he went to the doctor too late – but you know about that already.'

Muzz's grandad says something that sounds angry. Muzz doesn't translate.

'What was that, Muzz?'

'He says he wants me to say just what he says.' Muzz shrugs. 'Fair enough.'

Muzz's grandad speaks again.

'He says he has learnt that people hating and being divided is no good. He wants you to know that when he was young he fell in love with a girl – I can't believe he's saying this, Ellie – but his parents refused to let them marry. She was a Sikh: wrong religion. Six months later his father is dead, fleeing to Pakistan because Muslims and Hindus don't want to live in the same country. He says hating is no good – yes, well, he's told us that already.'

Muzz's grandad says something else, then stops for Muzz to translate, but he doesn't; Muzz just sits there looking embarrassed. His grandad speaks to him and Muzz answers back; in no time they're having what looks like a blazing row. His grandad wins obviously; Muzz stares at the floor.

'*Acha*,' he says. '*Acha*. Okay, Grandad.'

Muzz takes a breath. 'He says he should have been allowed to marry the Sikh girl. He says he knows I am reluctant to marry Bushra and – how embarrassing is this! – he gives you and me his blessing to get married!'

I laugh out loud, can't help myself, and then immediately feel bad: this guy's grandson has just been murdered and I'm laughing in his face. I hope he thinks I'm laughing through surprised delight.

'But Muzz, tell him it's a complete non-starter!'

And immediately feel bad for Muzz – was it such a ridiculous idea from his point of view?

'I already have!' says Muzz. 'What d'you think we were shouting about?'

'I dunno! I'm just sitting here having my future discussed by two blokes in a language I can't speak. Feels kind of weird.'

Muzz's grandad is staring at me.

I have a Romeo and Juliet moment: me and Muzz together, an item, the bridge across the divided communities, putting an end to the race war, the thing that heals the town. It's a story I'd like to believe, I'd like to be in, but I can't. And anyway, it couldn't really be Romeo and Juliet because Muzz's grandad, far from disapproving is staring at me with his eager eyes, wanting this to happen.

I'm sorry Imran is dead, but I can't do this. Romeo and Juliet is a story, and your grandson is my good friend, and that's all.

'Muzz,' I say, 'you know what's what. We've never laid a finger on each other and no way are we going to start now. Tell him.'

'I already have. He's not too good at listening.'

'Tell him again. Tell him as far as I'm concerned you can marry Bushra if you want.'

'That's not going to happen now. He knows it's a bad idea. I think he just liked the idea of Muzz marrying a nice girl from back home.'

'Poor girl,' I say. 'Lucky escape for her!'

'Snap!' he says. 'Me too. Who wants to get married?'

He can't see that from his grandad's point of view Muzz is his last hope.

The over-ripe melons behind his grandad look like collapsing heads, and they're putting out a stifling scent that's starting to make me feel sick.

'Tell him I'm sorry about Imran, Angi is, we all are, but tell him there's nothing I can do to make things right. Tell him, Muzz!'

And I go.

2

My toes are starting to hurt but I'm going to prolong this moment because I won't be doing it much more. Get to a certain age and standing on your bedend with your head out of the skylight becomes a bit uncool, doesn't it?

From up here you can't see them but in the street there are some council officials walking about with clipboards, the start of the inquiry into 'the disturbances'. They point at things and discuss them – the CCTV cameras, the boarded-up windows, the knocked-over traffic bollard, even the grate in the road outside our shop; you'd think they were explorers seeing the pyramids for the first time. They wear these isn't-this-an-interesting-part-of-town smiles but we'll never see them again, and the inquiry will decide something or other. I've come up here to get out of the way.

I'm doing my own inquiry, and when I've worked out what happened, who did what, I'll write it up in the minutes book. But I'm not ready yet.

When they came to clear up all the broken glass I went and knocked on Mrs Pearl's door, in case she wanted to stop them, but she wasn't in.

I said to the two men sweeping up: 'There's diamonds mixed in with that glass.'

They laughed, and one of them said: 'Yes, and I'm the Pope,' and they just carried on.

Matty's got a new brum-brum, and Angi says that Lewis has a new girlfriend. Well, I've seen the new brum-brum, but I don't know when we'll see Lewis's new girlfriend.

Angi isn't seeing anyone right now. She says she misses Imran too much, which is a first for her because she usually goes on to the next one without batting an eyelid. They've finally released Imran's body and the funeral's tomorrow. Muzz says the tradition is only men go to the burial itself. Anna said: 'Let them stop us!'

I'll have to go down. I don't want to, in fact I'd like to stay up here for ever, but my feet are killing me. Time to say ta-ra to the chimneys and the pigeons.

But I'm just starting to pull my head in through the skylight when something amazing happens: the black binbag comes loose from the TV aerial.

The breeze must have shifted direction or the plastic must have torn, I don't care; all I know is that this black thing which has been snapping and crackling angrily for months and months lifts free of the aerial and floats away over the rooftops, and it makes me feel so happy I want to shout at the top of my voice. I don't, of course, just watch it get smaller and smaller as it drifts away towards those distant hills. Maybe I will go there one day.

I climb down off the bedend with a big grin on my face. So how do you explain that, then?

3

Brian's agreed to take us to the graveyard on condition that we keep our distance and wait till the burial's all over and everyone's gone before we go near. Anna says it's stupid that women aren't allowed but I can see she doesn't want to make an issue of it, not today.

Angi's decided not to come. She says she doesn't want to think of Imran in the ground, covered with earth, so she stays behind as Anna, Diarmid and me climb into Brian's car.

I've tried to imagine what Angi feels about the chain of events that led here, events that only she, Imran, Lewis and me know about, that she can't share with all the people who are watching from their doorways as the hearse prepares to leave.

Not Imran, any more, he doesn't know anything now.

She feels – what? Special? Guilty? Bereaved? Maybe she thought this one was going to work? Maybe it would have, I don't know.

But of course there wasn't 'a chain of events': whoever killed Imran were probably just racists who picked on him at random, just another Asian taxi driver. I'd almost prefer it if they'd been friends of Lewis who did it in retaliation, at least there would have been some logic behind it, not this senseless murder, this brainless idiocy. Sometimes I have to shut my thoughts off because they don't get me anywhere.

'Looks like we're ready to go!' says Brian starting the engine.

'Where is it, the graveyard?' asks Diarmid in the passenger seat.

'Haven't got the foggiest,' says Brian. 'We're playing follow-my-leader here.'

We're the last of the cars following the hearse as it glides slowly through the town. At one point we're nearly separated from the rest by the traffic lights but Brian drives through on red, chuckling to himself.

'Just let them try to stop us; funerals means different rules!'

Anna rolls her eyes and sinks down in her seat so she can't be seen.

'Oh, yeah!' she says. 'The special Brian-can-drive-through-red-lights rule! Try telling the judge.'

The line of cars starts to climb out of town towards the windfarm.

'Strange,' says Brian. 'Looks like we're going to you-know-where.'

The ruined church appears on the skyline.

'Hey!' says Anna sitting up. 'Our favourite cemetery; great!'

The hearse and the other cars pull up, but Brian passes them and drives further up the hill before we stop too, next to a stile, and park up.

We walk in single file along a path that takes us across the moor towards the windmills. These turning blades are steady and reassuring, unlike the helicopter rotors, and their gentle *shush* doesn't even drown out the bird-song. We sit in the heather and look down on the procession of men, most of them in white, following the coffin into the graveyard. Our friends, the two rooks, perch on the ruined roof of the little church and oversee operations, cawing in encouragement.

A small figure in white waves at us: Muzz. Anna and I wave back. I can recognise his grandad, too, with his red beard, but he's not going to wave.

'So where's the grave?' asks Brian.

Good point: all we can see down there are old gravestones, the ones we searched through looking for Christy and Connor, but there's no sign of a hole dug ready for today. But then the procession thins down and we can see that it's filing through a gate out of the main graveyard. The coffin has a bumpy ride going through the narrow gate.

We can't see clearly what happens when the procession has gone through the gate, some dark green trees block the view, but the white figures come to a halt.

'That must be the Muslim bit,' says Diarmid. 'Separate from the old Christian bit.'

'It figures,' says Anna. 'You'd think dead people could all be dead together, but no. Too simple, that.'

'It doesn't look like they bury Christians up here any more,' says Brian. 'And anyway, cremation's all the rage these days.'

'What do you want to be when you grow up, Diarmid? Buried or cremated?' says Anna.

'I'm going to leave my body to science,' he says.

'Do you think they'll want it?' says Anna.

'Medical students need to practise on something,' says Diarmid, a bit serious and sensible.

We wait for the mourners to come out from behind the trees. Brian realises it's not heather we're sitting on but bilberry bushes. He starts picking them, storing them in the palm of his hand until he's got too many and then tries to persuade Diarmid, unsuccessfully, to give him his baseball cap to store them in, so he eats them instead, making his tongue purple and showing it to us. It passes the time.

The white figures start to wander back into the main graveyard. Muzz breaks free from the rest of them, climbs over the wall, and comes up the hill towards us, his whites flapping.

'Hi, guys!' he says, breathless from the climb. 'All over. 'Bye 'bye, Imran.'

Anna, tough-nut Anna, hard-as-nails Anna, bursts into tears. Brian makes sympathetic noises, and Diarmid pats her arm a couple of times and she calms down a bit.

I say: 'Am I allowed to go to the grave now, Muzz?'

'Why not? If anyone dun't like it, they'll say. They're all going anyway,' he says. 'But there's nothing much to see; no gravestone yet.'

'All the same,' I say.

And I set off down the hill, Brian and Diarmid after me.

It's not surprising we didn't see the gate into the other part of the graveyard last time; it's hidden by a Victorian tomb that must have cost a bomb. Still, if you're dead and you've still got piles of money, you might as well splash out on where you'll be spending eternity.

Diarmid was right, the new bit under the trees is the Muslim graveyard. There are a dozen or so gravestones, all quite new, with Punjabi or Arabic on them as well as English, and at the end of the row, two guys shovelling earth into a hole.

That's it, that's Imran in there.

I swallow.

And that's all there is, in the end.

But you can't stare at a pile of earth for very long. Diarmid and Brian wander off and I look to see if I recognise any of the names on the other graves. I don't, but I notice on some gravestones the Arabic writing overlaps with the English, which is a bit odd.

Then I realise of course it doesn't 'overlap' and it's not Arabic; it's someone with a spraycan. Graffiti.

I'm past words.

Diarmid calls: 'Dad, come and look at this.'

He's by the wall that encircles the graveyard, squatting down close to the wall. We go over to him.

'Look!'

He points at a gravestone which is set into the wall. It is covered in grey-blue lichen and the writing has nearly worn off in places, exactly how gravestones are meant to be.

Finbar
d. 1856
Fintan
d. 1857
Outcasts from the land of their birth
Outcasts from their Church
Brothers re-united
This stone is placed here by those who loved them

'It's them!' says Diarmid. 'Except their names are wrong.'

I say: 'How can it be them if their names are wrong?'

Brian says: 'Who said their names were Connor and Christy in the first place?'

'You did!' I say.

'I never!'

And now I don't know.

'Doesn't matter,' says Diarmid. 'It could be them. My great-great-great grandad, one of them is, probably.'

'Makes you feel proud!' says Brian. 'And look at what it says: 'Outcasts from their land'. Outcasts even from the official bloody graveyard!'

I feel a little shiver, standing among the long dead

we're not sure about, and the newly dead who isn't even properly covered yet, and the dead who somebody makes a special trip up from town to insult with a can of spraypaint.

'Let's go!' I say, and we walk back into the main graveyard and climb the hill towards Muzz and Anna.

The ground is rough so I'm watching my step, till halfway up the hill I stop and look ahead.

Anna and Muzz are kissing.

Now, where did that come from? How long has it been going on? How come I didn't know about it?

I feel puzzled and stupid, and look round at Diarmid and Brian climbing the hill behind me, but they don't look up, just keep going. Did they know? Surely not; I can't be the only one in the dark!

But then, the puzzlement starts to fade, and it's okay: my two best friends, doing whatever they feel like. It's okay. Behind Anna and Muzz, the windmills are waving their arms and cheering. Everything's okay.

Everything in my minute book so far has been miserable; sad stories from the past. The next story in it is going to be happy: Anna and Muzz's story. I'll write it before it happens, just to make sure it's happy.

We walk back to the car, Anna and Muzz in front. Muzz has little red stains on his back from lying on the bilberries.

Nobody speaks.

Note

Thanks are due to all the friends, especially the young adults, who have taken time to read drafts of *Victory Street* and make it a better book.

Particular thanks to Thea Hurst, who witnessed Kristallnacht as a child and remembers with affection the Italian ice-cream shop which continued to serve her after other shops refused because she was Jewish. *Thea's Diary: Leipzig, Warsaw, London* is published is Germany and used in schools there.

Thanks also to the *Lancashire Evening Telegraph* for permission to print the following extracts.

When the inquiries into the riots in the northern English towns presented their reports at the end of 2001, the local newspaper ran a pair of front page pictures, one showing Asian people, one showing white people. The caption read:

> SEPARATE LIVES: Yesterday's reports portrayed a Britain where the Asian and white communities have little contact with each other.

The following week, the newspaper printed an apology, saying that relatives of one of the white children in the photograph

> have asked us to point out that her family includes people of both Asian and Chinese origin. We are pleased to make clear that she and her family enjoy good relations with people of all racial origins…

Victory Street is dedicated to all those people who, in spite of efforts to divide them, are able to play, live, work with and to love others, whatever their racial origins.